The Scrolls Of Kislev

Based on a true story

Novel

Nassar Al-Hassan

Middle East Director and Editor: Ahmed Shalaby
Cover design: Mahmoud Assad
Translation: Sania Nemer Yassin

AEEH PRESS INC

Nassar Al-Hassan's writings are distinguished by the diversity of complex identities, including the swing between multiple affiliations. He came in style full of meaning while preserving all the symbolic connotations that give him more than one reading. They rebel against the usual ideas that have a monotonous rhythm, and this is the role of existing literature that seeks credibility away from national, national, and religious bidding.

The journalistic work enabled the writer to see many strange personalities, and he had previously published many articles and short stories in newspapers and magazines that focused on the repercussions of external and internal conflicts of human beings and prompted him to be acquainted with many human experiences and transmitted through the lips secretly and publicly. His blending of reality with imagination contributed To enriching his stories with more credibility and making them realistic and logical. His selection of clear and profound vocabulary highlighted the ideas and features of the theme of the topics raised in his texts, with a rich narration of exciting events and stories.

His novels focused on highlighting the secrets and contradictions of society, and he worked to present them with complete neutrality, away from any affiliation and loyalty to any religion, belief, or partisanship of an idea. It was an honest mirror of the important events and a realistic and accurate monitoring of human psychology.

The **scrolls of Kislev** account for the painful events that took place in Syria, especially what accompanied the period known as the Safar *'Berlik famines'* and the *massacres* between the two world wars.

While the novel / **Habanji** / deals with the repercussions of malicious reports on the individual and society through personalities who struggle with each other to reach their goals by various means within a time context that extends for half a century in which values and principles have been gradually and systematically absent.

A novel **/secrets /** which is in progress, dealing with the various issues of immigration and alienation of the members of the Arab communities and the repercussions of the sharp and eternal differences between the societies of the East and the West.

In the past, humans had been bisexual.

So God had divided them into halves to wander across the world, searching for one another.

Love is that desire to find the other who we had lost.

"Plato"

TABLE OF CONTENTS

Eroticism

It was the lack of time and his father's coughing sound that has saved her from his kisses with their bitter taste, which he has poured on her. She didn't want to spoil his happiness, but she also couldn't accept the repulsive and pungent smell of his mouth. They were indeed thanks' kisses and gratitude that he has tried to strengthen his love for her. Therefore, she accepted them at first, but she couldn't keep up with him by her acceptance as he drew nearer to her and tried to close his mouth to hers completely.

He has quickly got dressed with his father's coughing sound, which he used to wake everyone up early to get ready for the daily life chores. She took advantage of his going to take a shower to inspect their bed, which in its weird status and the contents of their bodily semen and almost revealed what they had done yesterday. It has been a long time since their last intimate encounter was completed with the usual pleasure and comfort. They were indeed able to quickly fulfill their desire from time to time, but it was more like an imperative duty to expel the excess of what was in their bodies of human instinct, in addition to what has bothered them from the necessity of self-control and caution and the imposition of complete silence so that no sound could be heard from the surrounding bodies exposing their actions. So, as soon as he had shut the door on them, he has rushed to her and he seemed to be a different person from what she had been accustomed to from him before a few moments ago. He just didn't take off his clothes but he also took off all of his shyness at once. At first, she was reticent of his blunt boldness, but as soon as his wonderful touches awakened her body, she became completely in tune with him.

Wonderful minutes they have spent together with complete adhesion and cohesion to their bodies soaked with love and fascination. His kisses were wonderful and bold, and they were able to penetrate what she couldn't say. His mouth has seemed to be wet and with a good smell, it's another mouth whose splendor had dissipated in the morning. She almost alerted him to this, but she was afraid that her words and frankness would anger him and dissipate the happiness that had followed their intimate encounter. She opted for silence and indifference, trying to convince herself that it was accidental and that would soon pass, and there was no reason to think about it more than it deserved.

She won't be able to forget last night easily, as it has contained so much that she could never forget. Their groans had risen despite their numerous and futile attempts to avoid it. Their vague words that have emanated from their mouth have overlapped, igniting more and more lust in their bodies, during which they exchanged a lot of muzzling with their hands so that nobody would be able to hear what was happening.

-   Blessed morning, groom.

The sentence has kept him away from his straying, so he turned to explore its source. It was Yahya[1], a childhood friend.

- Good morning. He answered him shyly and smiled: After a dozen of children you say blessed morning, what did this have to do with this?

- How did this have to do with this?! This is what we say to the groom after the first night of marriage. Mashallah[2], your face is a groom's face who has spent the whole night making love; your face is uttering everything.

---

[1] Translator: John.
[2] Translator: God willing.

- How are the children?

- Fine, but don't change the subject. So, how was your night of making love? Was it full of pleasure or half to half?

He has resumed his shy laughter with great reservation, for he knows Yahya's tongue and what would result from it if he spoke out. He was helped by Ibrahim's coming to join them, and the three hurried their steps to the nearby school where they were teaching.

The bathroom on the ground floor made it easy for her to sneak in to take a bath. A simple and old bathroom, the door of which can hardly let one person passing in, and at first glance it looks like a corroded stone cave.

She hurriedly began using her secret washing technique, which her husband had taught her when she complained to him of the problems she had suffered from, especially on severe cold days, which is summed up by simply wiping the body with a liter of water only, instead of wasting a lot of water. At first, it seemed difficult to her, and she replied to him: It's possible for men, but for women, we need ten liters of water to wash our hair alone.

On that day, he answered her that she should wipe her body only, as he did that without water, which was an excuse for him to make love with her again, and go further into her soft body.

The first time his idea didn't work but repeating that has taught her that a little water was enough to wash her body and the idea wasn't only to save water but to avoid the cold and shorten the time, as well as to avoid the suspicion that might creep into her mother-in-law's thoughts, as she was always keen on her friendliness. It's true that her mother-in-law is good and treated her like her daughter, but she didn't forget her mother's advice not to do any personal behavior in front of her that might provoke her jealousy as a female as much as possible, especially concerning the intimate relationship between her and her husband and everything that follows that.

He asked her for a cup of tea, she stopped feeding the baby to serve it to him.

- I swear by God, this world is weird and astonishing, Abu Fahd[3].

Abu Fahd has smiled despite the ambiguity of his wife's sentence and left her to do so.

- The Jews had expelled us from our homes and we had come to live in their homes; if it were up to me, I wouldn't replace our house orchard in all of this country.

Abu Fahd snorted as he was listening to her, for what had happened, in reality, no human mind could comprehend. While he was immersing in his reflections, Umm Fahd[4] rose up and quickly killed a crawling insect in the room corner.

- Woe to, this house is like an insects den. Umm Fahd said while she was about to kill another insect. Salma has quickly helped her and added:

- I have killed more than twenty insects today.

The house was infested with crawling insects, despite everyone watching them and ready to pounce on them. Abu Fahd went out to explore the place more, hoping to find the insect's den, releasing dozens of curses and killing as many of them as he could. He was

---

[3] Translator: Fahd's father.
[4] Translator: Fahd's mother.

disturbed by the walls' erosion, but his apprehension was from the strangely shaped pile of stones that seemed to be a huge den for these insects, despite his attempts to cover it with layers of mud he made from the small garden soil.

He went up to the upper floor, which consists of two rooms, only one of which is habitable, to explore the house courtyard and to close whatever holes he might find with that mud.

He forcefully threw a piece of clay into the hole that is equal to a palm-size and another next to it, and then sat down, exhausted, surveying the floor and plugging all the holes he had found. That old fear that had always stuck to him came back to him as he looked at his son's bed with apprehension and caution, and he remembered how one day he killed a scorpion that nearly stung Fahd in his childhood. That day he hit it more than once and even crushed it. He wasn't satisfied with that, so he burned it until he was certain of its death, despite his wife swore to him that he had killed it.

That day he didn't sleep, he checked on all the house corners and there was no advice he heard to ward off that danger but he did it. He might be a little exaggerated in his fear for his son, but his loss of his children while they were fetuses or immediately after their birth justified that for him.

When Umm Fahd aborted her first fetus, his peers winked to him that intimacy might do so, and he believed them. That night he has had sex several times, with lust and recklessness. He was a young man, and that was his only pleasure in life.

However, in her second pregnancy, she had left him completely and went to her family's house following their advice.

Nevertheless, she has aborted her fetus. Their neighbor, Umm Saad[5] has prescribed to her a foul drink, which made her vomiting several times until he took pity on her, so he approached her and hugged her to him. Umm Fahd was slender, of medium stature; he didn't know her previously, nor saw her until the wedding night, as was customary at that time.

Her abortion had been repeated, and after that, she has stopped being pregnant for several years, and then became pregnant and completed her pregnancy. Nevertheless, she gave birth to a dead fetus. On that day Abu Fahd cried a lot and for a long time.

He was unable to bury him with his hand, although he had embraced him to the cemetery, and the mourners could barely pull him by his arms to bury him. It was a hard and heavy night in which he didn't close his eyes, and neither did she. She was looking very pale and gloomy.

Everyone took pity on their deep and frequent grief, and daily visits began to increase to get them out of their grief.

Several abortions had followed, until that day when her sister came with an old woman, an expert in women's affairs, who gave her palatable oil, and fed her honey for several days with special foods, some of which seemed strange. She wiped her stomach with olive oil, while she was reciting in a low voice Qur'anic verses and desirable supplications. That day, her body calmed down, but her sister continued visiting and praying for her. The pregnancy wasn't difficult as she got used to it, but the fear of its continuation was the source of her concern. In recent months she lay down in bed motionless upon the old woman's advice. She was frightened as she embraced him while the assembled women were reading verses and supplications. One of

---

[5] Translator: Saad's mother.

them said: "Let his name be "Fahd"[6], so that the Angel of Death would mistake him for it." The audience unanimously had agreed on the suggestion's precision, thus they memorized his name and announced it.

The first days had passed with some anxiety, she carefully breastfed him, and her sister took turns taking care of him for the moment. They postponed his circumcision at first, for fear haunted them, even though he seemed to be in good health until one day he was forcibly taken from her bosom.

She cried while embracing him with all her tenderness after they brought him back to her to laugh the next day after he urinated in her sister's face as if he was punishing her for the feminine comments made from her when she saw the erection of his little genitals. He still keeps his circumcision wounds, but she went back to tell it to his father, despite her sister's request to keep it quiet to laugh together for a long time.

She let his hair growing in his childhood, and then cut it and asked her husband to pay charity equal to his hair weight, and he did, despite their difficult financial situation. She paid attention to her sister's notes that his crying sound was as strong as a leopard's howl, and she said that every person has a part of his name, so he's Fahd in word and deed.

Fahd released a distinctive voice after his second sip of the cup of tea and added:

Indeed, you're undisputedly the king of tea. Yahya smiled at the compliment sincerity, as he prides himself on his experience. Yahya was more than a friend, and despite he's a garrulous one and

---

⁶ Translator: Leopard.

not keeping secrets, he was good and gentle, and he was a good storyteller to the old stories he heard from his grandfather. Thus, his talk was very entertaining, and he also had the talent of stories' making up, to the point where reality was mixed with imagination and he had often listened to him on the way back while he was telling him his endless stories. When he was exaggerating in making up events, he looked at him with a direct and sharp look, and the eyes language might confirm the story's credibility or not.

Fahd's features were obvious to him through which he has known how he would complete the story. If Fahd's facial expressions indicated astonishment and doubt, he would stop immediately, to find another way out for his plot, or would pretend to forget, so that the story suddenly ends. One day, while they were near the cemetery, Yahya began telling a story about the dead and the other world, and the silence and the rocks surrounding the cemetery had added more horror to the story. So, he enjoyed watching Fahd's growing fear and terror. He was refreshed to see his friend engulfed in his gloomy and silence, but he stopped when Fahd began to speed up his steps to the point where   Yahya muffled his inner laughter and happiness in possessing that amazing ability and hid his pride so as not to lose his friendship, that friendship that was increasing between them day after day because of their keenness on that.

Yahya didn't hide anything from Fahd, and he's like that with everyone, he loosed his tongue, and then he regretted it the most.

Fahd would alert him sometimes and fix the critical situation at other times, and Yahya admitted that his tongue was the cause of all his problems, so Fahd was keen not to tell him everything and even justified to him one day after knowing what had precede and he hid it from him for fear of not concealing it.

Yahya wasn't the only child of his parents but was the youngest among several brothers and sisters, but his brothers' cruelty and harshness in dealing with him made him prefer Fahd on all of them. As for his sisters, they had quickly get married, and their visit became a story space for dozens of feminist stories that were overflowing with marital secrets in his absence, which he sometimes used to listen to be able to understand the stories cut out because they were ashamed to tell them in front of him. Then, he would give free rein to his imagination when he later recounted what he had heard to Fahd, but with a gesture and another plot.

Those tales weren't completely hidden from Fahd because he had heard some of them from his mother, so it was inevitable that Yahya had to make up another end for every story he heard to ensure that Fahd wouldn't interrupt him and claim that he knows it. Of course, their friendship wasn't without some inconveniences caused by some jealous people, but the days have soon revealed to them the falsity of that to reconcile again and for a third. Fahd adhered to Yahya with the moral advantages he had found in him, in addition to the kinship ties between their mothers.

Umm Fahd used to see in Yahya the brother she had always wished for her son, so his presence was a source of constant welcome, and this has eased her constant terror over him on his daily journey to complete his education, as his absence, no matter how short, was distasteful to the point that she preferred to sit with him even during his studies than anything else.

Many verses of poetry she had memorized because of his frequent repetition, to the extent that she drew his father's attention to the effect of what she had learned, and she kept comforting him with her presence until his marriage to withdraw from that usual scene.

Of course, it was strange at first for a young wife to sit for a long time to listen to what her husband had memorized; she praised his memory, but she quickly became addicted to him and became addicted to reading, which most of her female peers were deprived of.

This was their chance to be alone with each other, as the intimate touches have increased as he approached the end of his study with her.

I was ashamed when he caught me once, and I was peeping at his genitals, so he also approached shyly and whispered in my ear, his embarrassing questions to me despite my young age confused me, as he was like me yearning to discover me, so I matched him until my mother and my older sister's advice woke me up.

I've heard the word "you've exposed us" a thousand times. At first, it was my mother who said it, and then my sister followed her repeatedly, disapprovingly, to confirm her qualifications as a mature woman.

My looks were between excitement and curiosity, a body I had never familiarized myself with before, not to mention the wisdom and proverbs that my mother dropped in my ears before the wedding. I was confused that day and even looked like a helpless idiot.

Some women have intervened to remedy the spontaneous lapses I had committed, and then I realized that I had entered a different world, not because of the strangeness of the place or the characters, but because of what I had to do and live within it.

My sister rebuked me from looking at him and I thanked God that she wasn't among those whom my mother had chosen to talk to me away from her. They shyly and stuttering tried to explain what my mind doesn't accept. I admitted that I was shocked at that time.

Between a big rumble and my sister's sudden rebuking for my blunders, of course, they celebrated my little wedding.

Hours had passed while I was reviewing what I received; I looked at the joyful faces that brought me out with ululations and laughter from what I was in. The most wonderful of them were the old women, they were the ones who had brought me back to my childhood, and they were the closest to me in thought and logic, they have created that balance that I was needed on that difficult day.

I remember their laughter after hearing that I wanted to go to the toilet. I tried a lot to control myself until I felt that I was going to urinate on myself, so I screamed with fear from the looks of my sister who was watching me, but what should I do in a situation like this?

"You've exposed us," my sister repeated dozens of times as she took my hand to the toilet while I was silent and with a lower head. When I came back, my mother-in-law rushed to embrace me with the tenderness that I was in dire need of. She laughed at me and repeated all the words of compliments she knew. Then, the women shrieked successively the ululations, while looking at me and kissing me passionately.

I was annoyed by some thick lips that sucked my tender cheeks. I have indeed attended many weddings before, but when I'm the bride, the matter is completely different, and what would come after would be more surprising and weird. Despite the long hours they spent explaining what I'm about to do and their simplification, I was lost that day and that wandering was increasing and increasing.

Fahd shut the door on us, and the successive ululations outside had eased my fear, which escalated as he approached me. The ululating shrieked again with enthusiasm and harmony, sending us the encouragement we needed as if it were a hidden pat on our bodies.

I initially gave in to what was to come. He touched my palm and kissed it, so I rose and moved away from him a little, following their advice. I didn't hear his laugh, but I realized it by myself. Their instructions were contradictory, so I would shake up sometimes when I remembered that torrent of them. I spent the first moments between shy away and reluctance, while I was being like him, wishing to explore the other body. He gently and rationally went on kissing my body with his lips, which as soon as it responds his body cells would shrink and contract by orders from my tired memory. I used to push him with my hand and he would kiss and accept it and kiss my head and forehead again until it was difficult for me to count the number of his passionate kisses. He stopped several times in response to my denial of him, but the ululations quickly escalated to spread enthusiasm and love in his body again. His lips managed my lips, and amid my forgetfulness of the prohibitions, I completely surrendered to him, and he went ahead through my young body.

Everyone stared in amazement at the new guest who Fahd had embraced.

- A cat!!! The mother screamed weirdly while the children rushed to get around her, so she ran away from them.

Cats weren't strange to them, but their black color had irritated the mother.

- Why did you bring it a black cat? His mother wondered with astonishment.

- To stalk the enemies and eat them all. He answered with a smile.

Umm Fahd pressed her lips together, and then stretched them all at once. She added:

- Not all cats can do this.

- Mum, black or white, everyone is God's creation.

Umm Fahd feared everything, so she stopped to do complete many actions for fear of presumed apprehension. The cat quickly became accustomed to the house and began to roam around freely, while Umm Fahd shivered from time to time. She kicked her more than once with her foot when approaching her.

- This cat's shape jerks the body. Umm Fahd murmured, and she added: This is what we were missing!!! This black cat came to complete our horror in this house. Abu Fahd couldn't hide his laughter.

- Oh, woman, open your mind. This cat had distracted the children from you a little.

- What do you think if we go back to Palestine and live in our home? Umm Fahd asked.

- As I see you, we'll go back, we'll go back, and we need some patience. Abu Fahd said with optimism. Umm Fahd closed her eyes and murmured: Inshallah[7]… Inshallah.

She had a lot of painful memories, a tape in which all the events had overlapped. She tried in vain to keep them away from her, but they continued and continued… For a moment she seemed to be in another world where she had recalled that difficult path through the hills and valleys. A crowd of people stretched to no end, everyone in it was going on in complete ignorance of what was going on and what would go to happen.

It's the first maze that had felt after leaving their country. Aunty, aunty, Salma alerted her while offering her a cup of tea. Salma was more than a daughter-in-law to her, not because she had chosen her, but because she had found in her the daughter she had always

---

[7] Translator: God willing.

wished for and with her, the smile returned to their home, and the ululations had risen with each new birth. She indeed aborted more than once, but she was beyond that with a subsequent pregnancy.

She was the daughter and the friend, although she sometimes disagreed with her like all women. Salma might quickly apologize to her regardless of what they have disagreed on. This was what pleased her and brought her closer to her more, but the truth is that she was like a mother to her and many times she stood by her side in marital quarrels, which were rarely occurring in the home, which began to renounce sorrows little by little.

Yahya has surprised him with a strangely shaped piece of silver, which he has quickly hid with a white rag. Then, he began his speech, unleashing a torrent of oaths as he was accustomed to. He didn't comment on what Fahd said about the taste of tea, but instead showed him again that silver piece and began explaining in detail as usual. Although Fahd's looks were normal, they seemed vague to Yahya, so he went back to explain to him how he had found another basement that leads to the first basement.

Fahd contemplated the piece while listening to his friend. It was a simple piece, but was old, with deep inscriptions in it. He worked hard to decipher its talismans, but he couldn't. He added one word: Jews.

Yahya replied: That is, by God, Jews.

At his intense urgency, he descended with him the eroded stone staircase. The basement leads to another basement, where he had found the silver piece. He returned to contemplate and search the basement corners, hoping to find more of it. They spent some time and Yahya found out the walls and floor of the mysterious basement, while Fahd stood contemplating, like him, the narrow space with its secrets and mysteries. Yahya unleashed his fertile imagination and had begun a series of speculations to explain everything he had witnessed. They hurried out so as not to draw more attention to them, as several families were sharing their housing in this large house. This visit raised vaguely many questions in himself of what he saw, so on his way, to his house, he was contemplating the stone arches, paintings, and inscriptions that topped the adjacent houses' doors.

He came into the house with silent steps and rolled into the bed with a thousand questions in his head. The bed tightness caused compulsive friction with his wife's body. He was in dire need of this warmth to get him out of it. Salma made up a false nap to increase her enjoyment of his fingertips' touch and the warmth of his body. It wasn't the first time that she was drowning in the pleasure of rubbing his body against hers, while he was embracing her from behind. This position took away the monotonous repetition boredom of the intimate relationship between them and also spread in their bodies the delicious numbness that followed. She often surrendered to him to tamper with her as he wanted, as relaxing to the palm of an expert in her body was her periodic pleasure that she used to according to a regular sensory harmony between his body cells and hers. When he did it the first time, she lay down to his left arm with her thick and bouncy hair. She fell asleep until he woke her up again with his warm body.

Her young age has forgiven her many mistakes as well as her spontaneity and kindness which he needed them.

The murmurs that reached my ears frightened me, and I cautiously proceeded to find them out, because they were coming from that empty room. I muffled my footsteps, even though the voices still overlapping in my ears. My right foot suddenly stiffened, and the other stiffened after I realized that I know them well.

I was so close to the extent that I could distinguish the sounds well. I quickly retreated after watching them together; I almost burst out laughing at that scene that followed my fear and apprehension.

I quickly withdrew for fear that one of the children would wake up, so I didn't want to look like someone was peeping at them. Now I'm sure it's hereditary genes those voices that rise from Fahd in the last third of the intercourse. I wasn't amazed at the place I had caught them, but because I thought they had passed it long ago.

I tried to find out the children's condition; they were all asleep, so I rushed to Fahd for fear that he would see what I saw if he had to go down to the toilet. He was asleep, as usual, after he completely consumed his body in the intercourse, and then fell into a deep sleep. Sometimes I'm indeed the one, who caused this, but he often was the one who insisted on the next rounds between us, and despite the advice I received earlier, my body forced me to touch his body to urge him to stay in my arms. I used to hide my eroticism in his body and often hugged him from behind after I was sure of his nap, to get with his warmth the orgasm that flew me high.

Oh, my naivety! How did I think that my father-in-law had retired sexually, and he's this valiant knight's father? Minutes passed and I was recalling what I had seen in that hidden corner. In fact, life is full of scenes that explain the creation's simplicity. Poor my father-in-law, how he could do that in such a difficult place? It was a small room that seemed to have been neglected after its construction until it had become this way.

Oh, my naivety! How many times have I seen him check it out, trying to fix it, despite the difficulty of doing so alone? Our selfishness had reached such an extent that we didn't care about their hidden emotional needs, and we let them share their bedroom with the children. Now I understand the reason for her taking her bed away from him so that she would sleep on the east side and he would sleep on the west side. The children were her soul, and she was everything to them. From the beginning, she did that and I accepted it. As soon as I would finish nursing my child, she would take him in her arms for hours and hours.

I thought it was an emergency because she longed for motherhood, but continued with every child I gave birth. I had just to get pregnant and breastfeed and she took care of all the rest. I didn't deny that I have once complained about this situation, and even I tried to indirectly incite my husband against her, but I regretted it after that and cried for a long time, but soon I would come to kiss her and ask for her forgiveness. I had never imagined this poor woman might do what we did. There is no doubt that she did it under force, what I heard, were individual groans from him that overlapped with her forcibly muffled moans.

My husband has used to sleep and I went with my fantasies because of those books he used to read to me at the beginning, and then he taught me to read them until I've got addicted to them.

I used to see him with his head bowed, except for her large, round buttocks. He followed her spontaneously, and vaguely. Those buttocks kept her away from touching him while they were sleeping, lest his desire escalate more and more and the children wake up to what they might do.

My mother-in-law resumed her complaint and suspicion about the black cat and her husband supported her after he saw strange movements on the house's southern wall adjacent to ours, and to make matters worse, one of the curious told us that house story to increase our anxiety more and more.

We concealed from my mother-in-law some of what we had known and brought another beautiful and smaller cat in preparation for keeping the black cat away from us due to the children's attachment to him. I wished we hadn't done as soon as the little cat came out for a while; he came back in pain from what the black, reckless cat had caused him. We tried to catch him but were unsuccessful as if he realized in his animal instinct that we were preparing to dispense with his services. I was wondering as I watched his annoying movements, or is it possible that he's this smart?

He stood there where we couldn't reach him, not even if we would throw small stones at him. He has provoked all of us despite our repeated attempts to disregard him at times or catch him at other times.

My father-in-law asked for my husband's help in repairing that small room, so I chose to remain silent for fear of revealing my peeping on them. Fahd agreed and spent his day off, transporting the necessary building materials to renovate the room. I checked what they did, and found that it still needed a lot before the job could be done. After they got tired, they sat down to share our lunch.

We couldn't hire a laborer and had to keep secret our repairs fearing being kicked out of the house. My husband and his father had to use those stones in the house courtyard as the black cat's meow escalated in defense of his ethereal corner. My mother-in-law asked them to stop, terrified of that cat's movements and sounds, so they stopped. My mother-in-law removed some of the scattered small stones in the garden basin and began digging up the soil in preparation for the planting of the bushes that my husband had promised her. They gave the place beauty and serenity. Everything had got better little by little, except for that damn cat and his weird behavior on that pile of stones.

My mother-in-law insisted that he was enchanted and was possessed by the jinn. Sometimes we laughed and thought about what she was saying, and at other times we had a strange shiver. We fixed the room and it became completely ready to receive their love with its renewed taste despite its age. I pretended idiocy as they moved their beds with the certainty that they would do it again and again in the dark night.

We were all suspicious of that pile, so I stayed away from it, especially after it was revealed to us more, and if it hadn't been for my mother-in-law's insistence on stopping the work, they would have been able, with the remaining stones, to restore some of the house walls. I didn't hear any murmurs while I was passing to the toilet next to the new nest, perhaps due to the distance between the intimate encounters between them, and this was confirmed by my mother-in-law who returned to sleep in the children's room without giving any reason. I understood her vague behavior from her future results, as she didn't show any reaction so as not to occupy herself too much with her fleeting visits to the love room. It was indeed said, "A woman only understands a woman." I learned a lot from her perhaps because I had to learn then.

That knowledge stream began to increase from the wisdom that my mother-in-law repeated cheerfully and succinctly, according to the situation she was in, and what my husband used to tell me from his daily observations and the books he brought us. I accepted the idea of learning in submission to his will to do so, and then I loved it because it showed me the other side of life, and even seemed more logical in its treatment of our various affairs than what we used to hear as a common custom. I suggested to him that we exchange our room for theirs, but he refused and justified by the difficulty of their ascent and descent of the corroded stairs. I didn't realize at that time his other intentions, which I later realized. We women, our actions and responses are spontaneously simple in some things. I forgot his ecstasy after he filled his lungs with a deep inhale after finishing the intercourse and lying down on his back and spreading his hands as much as he could.

I also forgot his voice loudness with rising lust until I had to mute his voice with my palm, which reprimanded me after receiving a strong bite from him. I thought his reaction would be the same as my reaction when he did it to me before, I also had those moments when my body screams in pleasure. I was at that time new to the fun and it was a beautiful day in which I had the pleasure, followed by a delicious encounter that exuded delights. I couldn't hide my groans despite my repeated attempts, so they set off, or rather they escaped me. He quickly closed my little mouth with his huge palm and continued to flow relentlessly inside me. I never asked him why he did that because I know that his family is with us at home and the sound may reach their ears. Nonetheless, we've already done it. That day when he showed them the white rag with my virginity blood and some of his semen, it seemed that the matter was different!

There were many unanswered questions in our customs, and the strangest thing was their condensation to create an eternal waste for our future generations, and then to bring out these contradictory accumulations in the form of strange and reprehensible actions, which I didn't familiarize with Fahd or his family.

How much I thanked and praised God while I was listening to the young girl's story like me who her husband foolishly surprised her with a scene of his genitals which was very ready and erected, so she fainted due to the horror of what she saw!

These questions were constantly recurring to me with every vague act I encounter. The peeping wasn't my habit, but as my mother-in-law sometimes sleeps in the second room, so this was forcing me to check the children's status more often throughout their sleeping.

I indeed listened to some love songs between them, but it was unintentionally from me. I hoped that she would respond to him and warm him always with her love because the next day he seemed more cheerful and bright, and she was as well, so this was giving us a lot of happiness. However, she soon would return to sleep next to the children, for a reason for which I didn't understand. Is it shyness from us..? Maybe and maybe something else we don't know.

I'm used to some of the jokes that my father-in-law was telling, even if he was very reserved in narrating any topic that my mother-in-law might get angry about because she quickly gives him a warning look and reminds him that she's present, so he shuts up briefly, and she rewards him later with a night in which she absorbs his angry feelings.

She was jealous, but I didn't notice this except during that difficult journey after we left our home. She often searched for him even if he went to the toilet away from the eyes. If I could erase something from my memory, it would have been the days when we used to walk and walk, as if we were lost in mystery. We were hungry, thirsty, and the endless fatigue in the unknown surrounded us and always follows us. Dozens of conversations were mixed without an answer and everyone was in an astonishment state.

We thought that we had run away from the actions and massacres that had been promoted to terrify us, to take a path more painful than death. We stopped after the march had exhausted the children and the elderly to notice that the numbers were more increasing. Queues of people all over the horizon had asked unanswered questions in difficult situations.

Al Kharab Neighborhood [8]

My mother-in-law was completely fed up when she heard that the neighborhood name in which we lived is: "Al-Kharab Neighborhood." [9]

She said: Oh, my son. It is right next to a house that was burned down and destroyed, and the whole house is strange, and in addition, you've brought me a black cat to upset me more! Why my son? And in addition it's among the Jews!!!..., didn't it remain in the Levant except for this house?

She finished her speech with some humor so as not to burden him more. As usual, my husband answered her with the smile of satisfaction that she was accustomed to. She vented her anger by throwing stones at the black cat that she collected from here and there to help when necessary. The cat didn't stop digging up the dust that rose in his ethereal place. Sometimes, I thought he did it to annoy my mother-in-law, and other times I saw him drowning in this ambiguous act. I also almost asked my husband to find another house for us, despite what we had done to fix it and I know that is so difficult to find another one.

We used all means to catch him, but all were in vain, even the trap that Fahd set for him took the life of the kitten. It was a sad day for the children, especially when Fahd took him out from among them;

---

[8] Translator: currently is Al-Ameen neighborhood.
[9] Translator: the ruin neighborhood.

they gave him pained looks and tears held captive by the eldest of them and generous by the youngest. This gloom was dispelled by a large cat, which crept up against the corroded wall of the house next to ours. The children threw him some of the food that he had devoured in a hurry, and they gave him more and more. His acquaintance with the children didn't last long, and he quickly frequented them with intelligence and cunning, even my mother-in-law accepted him with an uncharacteristic welcome.

The black cat has disappeared at first, but he came back to the wall and digging up the dirt again. We woke up terrified to a sound we didn't know; it was a bloody struggle between the black cat and the guest cat. Their violent rounds, full of sounds and fights, were repeated, while my mother-in-law stood looking with pleasure at the continuous retreat of the black cat, and his departure from us as a decisive result of the conflict between them. That day, after my mother-in-law realized that he left, she asked my husband to bring the sweets for celebration, and she added with a quiet laugh:

- I wish that God sends to the Jews such a cat and take them out of our country, and to be an irrevocable departure.

- Amen, Lord. We all spontaneously replied, Amen. It came out with one voice, in harmony with an exhale, followed by continuous collective laughter.

I didn't know whether it was his enormity or the pride of his victory that made his steps slow and monotonous, but what caught our attention was his repetition of the black cat actions from staying in the same place and exhuming dirt and small stones. My father-in-law caught his attention the cat's actions, so he suggested that we remove those stones to find out the matter. We all approved on his suggestion, except my mother-in-law who kept silent.

I helped them as much as I could that day, leaving the children to distract my mother-in-law from us for fear of snakes or scorpions. After we removed the dirt and the stones, a small iron plate appeared. After removing it, we found a lower basement. My husband slowly went down the stairs and checked the place, a few moments passed, and then he came back with a yellow and grimy face and asked us to hurry to help him to block the door. We helped him by putting some small and big stones on it.

Several days had passed, after which my father-in-law, Abu Fahd asked me to help him carry the elongated stones from that board, so I did, and he slowly descended into the basement. Then he went back to light the candle that suddenly went out. He lit it again and went down the stairs with faster steps, I expected that he would stay there for a long time, but he quickly came out with a gloomy face and strange looks similar to the ones that appeared on my husband's face last time.

We closed the door tightly and I preferred to keep silent, as the upset and frown status he was in, didn't allow any questions or conversations. In the following days, I was caught by their private conversations in a low voice and mutual facial expressions indicating the importance of the subject they were discussing. I was curious, but I had already accustomed myself to waiting until things became automatically clear, as the many questions and urgency may not necessarily result in an adequate or even correct answer.

I tried in my ways to understand what was going on between them, or what they saw in the basement, and the reason for the panic signs that appeared on their faces after they got out of it, but I could never do that. Several weeks had passed, and then my father-in-law went down to the mysterious basement and stayed there for a long time, and then come out with a bag he carried with him, but it seemed inflated after he gave it to my husband, who hurried his steps out of the house.

My father-in-law was exhausted and asked me to help him close tightly the basement hole. I did it and went back to my children looking for them, and trying to hide my astonishment after what I saw from them. Fahd returned to the house and was looking confused, so my father-in-law pushed him aside from my mother-in-law's gaze, who was preoccupied with the sweets she had prepared for the children. I asked them to join us to taste it; they ate with a clear appetite that I had never used to see from them like that.

It was a normal morning that followed that day as if nothing had happened. My father-in-law took his beloved coffee with audible and harmonious sips and then ate his humble breakfast. I was the only one who felt an idiocy state and straying after the brief reply I received from them, which didn't match their turbulent expressions at that time. I didn't know how they were able to hide this from my mother-in-law, who usually does not miss a few details, and even speculates about what will happen.

Where are you now? Where are your eyes that lurk in everything? Where are your ears that eavesdrops the finest whispers? My mother-in-law took me out of what I was in as if she knew that she had become one of the many questions that troubled me.

Several days had passed during which it caught my attention that the cat didn't do any of his strange behaviors as before. Or is it possible that what they took what was the cat looking for? But what was it? The black cat was also doing these suspicious movements, and if he stayed with us, he would probably refrain from them now. I couldn't hide it anymore, so I asked them many questions at our usual luncheon. They looked at me for a long time, and then they exchanged looks as if they had nothing to do with it. I wasn't accustomed to this secrecy from them. It seems that no matter how much we know around us, there remains a secret buried under wraps until it would be revealed for some reason one day.

I touched him more with my naked body and drowned him with those touches that he desired and my tongue almost utters the question that troubled me, but I shut my mouth until he completely got emptied his lust, while he's in my arms I trembled with his ecstasy several times and let out erotic groans unreservedly. I thought it was the right moment, so I surprised him with my question. His color has changed and curled himself up after covering his genitals with his small white towel. I also angrily grabbed my towel and in a hurry tried to get his semen out of my body. It's inconceivable that he withholds anything from me and divulges my depths secrets. I almost screamed at him that I wasn't aroused by his touches or kisses and that I yielded to him to do so.

- Please tell me before you sleep, what was that mysterious thing you pulled out from the basement?

His snoring has quickly clarified his condition to increase my fatigue amid dozens of speculations. I would have turned my buttocks for him to squeeze while he was cuddled with me if he had asked. I would caress him as he liked just to find out what he did.

I curled up next to him, hugging him more and more, hoping he would take pity on me and comfort me, or to find an answer in some of his body cells. I touched him more to find out what I wasn't used to his secrecy until I fell asleep with my dreams and nightmares.

The next morning, he told me, with his head bowed, pretending to hurry, that it was some remains that had to be disposed of.

I would have asked him: Does that short answer require all this deep thought? But he had been got out of the room. I didn't remember that he ever hidden anything from me. On the contrary, he informed me of everything, even his private writings, with his funny ideas. There is no corner that I don't know.

I purposefully and unintentionally dug up all the corners. He was an open book, and neither were his parents among those who love secrecy. Even his body I searched, I was young and thought it was a childish reciprocal game, I played it sometimes and he played it at other times. He would close his eyes completely to give me more courage to go with my touches, which started spontaneously and then became professional with his constant encouragement to me.

We used to close our room door under the pretext of sleeping early, to go to our game with its rounds. I didn't deny that I have enjoyed it more while he messed with my relaxed body in front of him, and we remained like this until my body became fatter and I could no longer lie down on my stomach, so he changed his plans in line with the new situation. I loved everything with him, for he was the one who introduced me to a new and interesting world which I found it in the books he used to borrow, to let me read with great eagerness, and then told him about them at length, so he returned the book without completing it, and he says to me with a laugh:

-        You spoiled the suspense that I wanted to read.

Perhaps it is one versus one of an old debt that he wants to get back now, I don't know. I tried to sneak into that mysterious basement, but I couldn't. All my attempts had failed. The days passed with their usual routine until a discussion raged between my husband and his father over getting a table out of the basement to use.

Of course, I supported my father-in-law, so that I might know some secrets or find an answer to what happened before. They brought out together an old wooden table that seemed sturdy and brought out some small things with it. Here my mother-in-law urged them to empty it and search in it for more useful things hoping to benefit from.

They alternately went into the basement and took out what each could carry. A lot of wooden and copper tools were scattered before us, some of which we had never seen before. I was amazed at a piece of beautiful medium-sized pottery in which the shape and color indicated its old age. I took it and found a lot of paper rolls with handwritten writings, and books and many other things were scattered here and there as well. I collected them and carried them to my room in a hurry while the rest were busy with what they found. I quickly went back hoping to find a sheet of paper or a newspaper here or there.

My mother-in-law didn't care about what I had found, only my husband was following my movements silently, and as I asked for, he went down to the basement for the last time in search of any book which he might reconcile me with. The scrolls shape and the container placed in pushed me to find them out. I sat contemplating them, touching and smelling them, and then I started reading them. A discussion has raged between my father-in-law and my mother-in-law about the use of pottery jars and the possibility of using them to preserve what we have. My father-in-law has argued that they are old and he didn't know what had happened to them in the past, while my mother-in-law saw that merely washing is enough to clean them completely from the dirt or even dirtiness that was stuck on them.

My father-in-law wasn't convinced and for the first time I saw him insist on his opinion, and my husband had always supported his father without expressing any reservation or even a third opinion. I didn't say a word; I left the whole discussion to them and tried to withdraw with what I had, to try to decipher the vague talismans. I tried my best to keep the scrolls order as they were and tried to find out their contents. They seemed strange in shape and content. Long hours had passed by and I was contemplating them. I set aside part of my time to retire there in the corner where I kept them in that old jar under the round table.

Every new word I had read has illuminated what I was ignorant of, so I hastened to read to learn more and more to reach a point that looked like a dark tunnel, so I read again. Who was that man?

I wondered while was looking at his contiguous and overlapping words, which sometimes were needed to be re-read a hundred times so that I can understand them.

Kislev, I'm Kislev, or Kislo, or Yusuf[10], as they like to call me, for the matter is the same for me; the important thing is that I'm the same and what I'm, whatever the letters of my name are on their lips. I spent a lot of my time alone. I was alone even when I was among them. It doesn't matter, I got used to it and it became a part of me. The obsession with writing had gotten to me along with what I heard from here and there about the mob actions that have spread and increased in the recent times, demanding that we have to leave from among them.

Why? I don't know. I want to write about my misery and the misfortune that has always haunted me like my shadow. Where are you, Dad?

Why did you leave me alone?

Where are you Jacob, O my master who surrounded me and protected me? How much I miss you, Dad, my friend... I wish I could write a poem for you that dispels my renewed loneliness and depression. You weren't only a father, you were everything.

I miss you; I miss your palm that patted my head and shoulder to remove my worries. I miss your shoulder, to rest my head on it and weep of their boundless injustice to me. I wish time had stopped when you held my hand and we roomed together in our journey through the lands of injustice that you bequeathed me.

Dad... you are the light flowing from all folds. How much I miss you, how much I'll miss you.

I longed to hug you and hear your voice, which is closest to a whisper, even in your anger. Who would read to me now? Who would

---

[10] Translator: Joseph.

tell me now the bedtime stories that I used to hear from you, and I still remember them in all their details?

Dad…Dad…

You were great in everything. O gentleman, even in your anger.

There isn't a day that I went through without recalling all the wonderful moments I spent near you, and quarreling with my memory to bring back to me all the details of your facial features and the laughter of your tired eyes from their evils.

Now I realize why you were calling me my friend, my friend. Now I repeat it in the same intermittent voice, with a rattle and pain, followed by a long weeping. In what language can I address you now?

Tell me, tell me to do.

In what ear can I hear you, and can my heart bear it?

They overpowered me when they took your coffin out of our house. Sorry, Dad, I couldn't stop them, they were many and I was alone.

Sorry, Dad, I didn't follow your advice to stay away, I fought with them and screamed and screamed to keep you with me, but they were many and they increased with my transcendent screams to you.

It wasn't an ordinary funeral day.

It was all the oppression.

It was all the injustice.

I fell on the ground motionless, I tried to gather myself and get up, but I couldn't, my rickety body betrayed me, even my body cells came out of me to stick to you. I took advantage of their inattention and came to you while you were lying down, so many hands tried to keep me away from you. I sipped my salty tears and swallowed my nose's flowing and bitter mucus, and the pain of losing you remained a lump that didn't retreat. They brought me back to consciousness more than once after I fell and hit my head on the ground.

There wasn't a day that passed that I didn't relive those bitter moments, which because of their frequent recurrence, I daily experience them. Memory is a constant pain, even if we recalled the most wonderful moments.

I forgot to ask you, my father: Couldn't you have postponed that difficult departure?

If you could waited for another day to tell me a new story, or joke that dissipates our pain, or even an inseparable silence in which I look long at you, and fall asleep to wake up, and look back at you, how much I longed for my memories with you, but without that day when they took out your body. I couldn't. How much I tried to banish that obnoxious part of my memory.

How much I tried to forget it or erase it from my memory, but it's there attached to the old pictures that come to me from time to time. All my attempts to divide my memory into a good part and a bad part have failed. It's a single sequential memory even though it's for different times that come back to me at the same moment and in a strange succession.

I'm Kislev, the boy who, despite all attempts, found it difficult to imitate his father. I'm Kislev, the lover of bread dipped in warm milk from my father's hand, and I chewed it unfailingly with my father's left palm, wiping what was stuck to the edges of my little mouth.

Where are you Sarah, why did you leave me here alone? I told you we could live somewhere else, but you believed them and didn't listen to me. I have done everything for you. I told you how much I love you.

I told you: Look at my eyes and examine them, then you put your hand on my chest to hear my love for you.

Here I'm writing all my life details, so that I can always read them and remember you, or for someone else to read it to know about us if God's will dictated that.

Yesterday I went up to the rooftop where we were meeting, I was jumping from it to your house rooftop after making sure that your mother came out. I remember those moments when we were stealing our burning love away from the eyes. I did everything you like. Why did you leave me, my love?

I'll write everything so that I can recall these memories there in our love corner to read and remember your beauty that you inherited from our grandfather Youssef, O glorious one.

I won't lose hope no matter how long it takes; I'll wait and write as if you are by my side talking to you face to face. Oh, how much is beautiful your charming face! How could someone saw it and forget it?

Slow are the days. Sometimes I get confused and I can no longer distinguish between them, I sneak out of them and look at the ground quickly with my steps to buy what I eat. I look to the sad and lonely citrus tree forcibly like me, we exchange our memories in silence, I transmit by it my longing for my father, and I throw food for the old turtle which suffers from her forced loneliness as well.

One day, I tried to get together the three of us, so I brought the turtle to the basin of the citrus tree and sat next to them, listening to the sound of her chewing the leaves. I contemplated her for more than an hour until she left me and went inside her shell for a reason I don't know, while the citrus tree remained silent as usual.

On my way to the kitchen to get a pot of tea, I heard mob voices outside. I felt that they approached the house, so I ran to the basement for fear of them. I could hear their screams with words threatening to kill us, the Jews. I closed the basement door and slept in it that night, it seemed to be safer, so I loved it; I felt it like a wonderful shell, so I spent most of my time into it after that.

I miss my memories with you, so I went up the stairs and wished I hadn't. Soon their stones fell on me, and they hit me until I almost fell down the stairs quickly to my safe shell. I sat back and remembered what happened, I never understood it. I brought the turtle in the evening to share my loneliness, but her noise disturbed me. I kept her for another night and then brought her back to the courtyard in the morning to do her usual routine.

It was a normal morning preceded by a disturbing night. I yearned for a glass of milk, so I went out early to buy it and came back to enjoy its taste with my old friend, the turtle with her old face. Forgive me; I stole that rug that I always loved. I jumped again on your house rooftop, took it, and put it in the basement with me as a memory of you. Do you remember it?

Do you remember the day I sipped your lips? It was a pleasant day and we secretly made love until we were awakened by your mother's simultaneous screaming by kicking me with all her might.

I no longer remember her many insults, except for the phrase that she repeated to me hundreds of times: You filthy bastard, you filthy bastard.

I was so freaked out that I almost threw myself off the rooftop, it was a hard time.

I have been afraid of your mother all my life. For the first time, your mother gave me a stern and spiteful look. I often moved away from her even before approaching me, for I was frightened of her face harsh features and her angry eyes movement for me.

I didn't expect her to come back so quickly that day so I jumped to see you and touch your wonderful hands. Maybe we had run out of time and didn't notice, or maybe she came back sooner than we expected. I was hit with dozens of successive and painful blows, especially the ones that hit my head until it made me run in the wrong direction. At first, I couldn't find a way out to escape from her, so I fell again and she tightened, hitting me with malice, and repeating:

"You're filthy bastard, you're filthy bastard."

Finally, I managed to escape and jump onto our house rooftop.

I went down the stairs at an unusual speed trying to hide in a corner, I thought she was following me behind me, I was panting and panting. I hid for a long time until I finally managed to get out.

Fortunately, my father was at that time outside the house, I didn't tell him what had happened. In the past, your mother used to stare at me with her frightening eyes, but after what happened, the word bastard was always repeated with her. I disregarded her a lot until that day when she severely hurt me, so I said to her: "I'm not a bastard," so she laughed with her mean face and said: "Ask your father."

I was surreptitiously climbing the rooftop, trying to peep at you, I was wondering what I was doing. My love for you that almost killed me and my hatred for your mother was unparalleled. With her ability to control things she was able to keep us away from each other and despite my complete avoidance of her, she was hunting for opportunities, so when she saw me she dropped her curses on me and certainly with that hateful word "bastard". Once my father heard her directing it to me, she quickly ran away from him. He hugged me and took me into the house. I tried to hide my tears from him, but he saw them, so he wiped them and kissed my forehead, and then smiled and said:

- You're my son. You're my son; don't care about her words.

I told him: But she always repeats it. Am I a bastard? Please tell me am I a bastard?

He smiled again, hugged me and said: You're my son. You're my son.

- But she always says that and some may believe her, as she's a midwife and has many acquaintances, but where did she bring this word from?

He didn't answer me and just hugged me. I tried to keep myself busy, but I couldn't avoid her more than once, and yet she often managed to stone me with that terrible word. I didn't find a solution but to resort to crying and exaggerating it in front of him, as the absolute confidence looks that she had when she uttered her malicious word made me suspicious of my father's brief answer.

My father realized that his repeated answers were incomplete and no longer convinced me, so one day he sat me next to him and held me with both hands. I saw his tired eyes containing me more and more as if he wanted to melt me in his body again to make me believe what he was going to say. Then, I was ashamed of myself when I had previously doubted this, his pulse and arteries were speaking the truth.

I wished him to cry but he didn't, old oppressive tears froze on his tired eyelids edges. He warmly said and in a low voice, I could hardly hear: You're my son, you're my son.

I said the truth no matter how loud and numerous were their lies. He stared at me so deeply that I thought his soul would enter my tired body as well. He said: I wished I hadn't told you about that, and I tried to avoid it, but it seems that there is no escape. You would be troubled by what you would hear, but it's the only answer to your questions. You're Kislev, this is the name that I gave you on the day you were born, not because I picked you up in that month as she told you that malicious one, but because you were born in it, and I had a dear friend in Istanbul whose name was Kislev, so I didn't hesitate to call you by this name, which seems unfamiliar when it's heard at the first time, but it means a lot to me.

They're sick illusions that only bred in her imagination, although the truth is completely different from that. It was a wonderful day..... But, it wasn't completed! I told you, my son, that what I hide from you is only to keep you away from the pain that would follow your knowledge of it. On that day, I had to find a nurse for you after your mother died of a fever that struck her right after you were born. It was a hard, painful day that I don't like to remember. This is what I hide from you.

I didn't want you to know about your mother's death after you were born. Anyway, it had been a long time since that, so don't worry.

Your mother was a wonderful woman, and I'll never forget her no matter how much time had passed, our marriage was quick and simple. Perhaps because of my previous acquaintance with her family, that had a good effect on our relationship, as we were neighbors in the same building after I settled in Istanbul. Her mother had quickly deepened her friendship with my ex-wife Isabella. That woman who made me suffer from daily escalating sadness and oppression, in addition to what I was suffering from the forced alienation pain from my city, Damascus, to my hard and tiring work as well.

It's a long and intertwined story, my son, previous events that I must tell you in sequence until you would understand them. He said this and kept silent, looking at me carefully. What beautiful feature of his face, which forces you to embrace him, so I embraced him.

He was sad while he was telling this story, so I let him complete it whatever he wanted. I also hated the sadness that mixed every character of his words. We drank tea and argued about other matters. I noticed the length of his hair, so I asked him to cut it. I felt his happiness as he lowered his head with keen silence to enjoy complete relaxation while having the haircut, which was confirmed by his only shaking his head in affirming, or negating to any question I asked, and I answered him with a muffled laugh.

My father was keen to keep me away from any difficult profession, in his opinion, harsh professions end in sickness and disease. So, one day he escorted me to a barber who is his friend, I know him well because we are one of his customers and he often visits us.

He greeted us with a usual frankness, and my father started his talk by suggesting that I work for him, therefore, as soon as he heard his approval, he talked in privacy to him on a topic that was circulating between them. My father listened to his words while I was *helping him to undress his clothes upper part so that his friend could perform him cupping. I sat close to them following the barber's exaggerated movements to teach me the first lesson. He took his transparent bottles one by one and put them on my father's back after he threw a burning cotton wick inside them. I expected to hear my father's pain screams, but he was satisfied by some shivering that followed the wick's touching his body.*

With quick blows from a sharp scalpel, the barber phlebotomized the dark blood of his back, along with his question accompanying those blows about any inconvenience or pain he had caused him. My father answered him negatively and urged him to phlebotomy more of his blood. The dark and strange color of blood terrified me. I stood next to him, holding his hand, watching the slowing down of bleeding drops. I kissed my father's hand after he softly pressed on it with his bowed head.

I noticed his spine's protruding bones, so I started touching them with my forefinger, so the barber Zaki winked me by a sign. My father sensed this because he doubled his pressure on my hand successively. No one understands me like him as if I was an open book for him to read easily.

How much I wished to ask him what is the secret that made him give me correct predictions, which I always tried to hide my questions so as not to embarrass him.

After the barber had wiped his body, they spoke in a low voice in the small room corner, and my father asked me to wait for him in the salon. I didn't understand at that time why the barber shut the door to the small room attached to the salon for a few minutes, but my father has explained it to me later. He needed an ointment to remove a boil in a sensitive area of his body. After that, the barber Zaki returned to dictate his work's terms, and of course, my father would be a witness to this.

My father knew that I abide by what I do, and he was the one who asked me to change the professions I have worked in previously without causing me any embarrassment with the employers. He did it himself and in his way. In fact, I didn't show any resentment from any decision he took because of my absolute certainty of his opinion rightness. He would often do this after he realized the hardship that had befallen me. He was certain that his work in construction was the most miserable, and he had talked a lot about this difficult profession, which had caused him many diseases and pains.

I had previously worked in the Coppersmiths Market for several months, in which I spent my time cleaning the small shop and doing what was asked of me. The coppersmith Azeez was sure of my complete discipline, so he gave me a copper piece to start working with under his supervision. His previous and subsequent remarks had confused me about every action I did, but I didn't disregard any of them.

The successive knocking sounds on copper plates were clicking in my ears even after I went back home, which made my father inform Mr. Azeez of my desire to quit work. I didn't object, not because of the work hardship, but because of the many remarks that Mr. Azeez gave it to me, which pours down upon me from the beginning of each day to its end, and his constant repetition of the same phrases until I memorized. His excessive eagerness to implement everything with utmost precision had confused me.

He was kind-hearted, but was eccentric, perhaps because of the copper hammers clamor in his head, or perhaps because of his old age, as he was over eighty years old. I whistled that day after he told me this, one day in his usual break after eating his simple meal. It was the most enjoyable hour of the whole day, especially if he began to remember the incidents that were still stuck in his memory. I got used to his interesting talk about the past, as I used to the insults series, that he used to say against women in the morning with his narration of what his wife had done.

At first, I sympathized with him with the convincing arguments he gave me, but I realized after dealing with him, that he is difficult to handle and has a fickle mood. I learned from his patience, and then the slow down when he contemplates any copper piece, in addition to a huge amount of wisdom and proverbs that he used to repeat in conjunction with what he does.

I used on my father's visit while I'm completely occupied with my work, I could feel him chasing me with his kind eyes in all my movements. I was standing for him respectfully and eagerly. My father wandered among the shop exhibits and then sat for a while next to Mr. Azeez for exchanging conversations. I was working while they were talking because I was completely confident that my father would tell me their conversation again in the evening after I returned home, which is what actually happened.

I was accustomed to my father's wonderful stories, which were extending and branching out day by day. When I sit next to him, he was telling me about what he went through, so I would try to imagine it. What he was telling was so impressive to the extent that it might bring me back between a dream and a waking life, so I was living it exactly as I imagined it.

My father wasn't happy with his hard and forced work; he was spending all the day working as a construction worker who was brought with others to build the palaces in Istanbul. Hard work for a little pay, and to complete the misery, a ruthless wife was waiting for him in the small room that he rented. She didn't stop complaining, groaning and lamenting the misfortune that put her in what she's in.

He became accustomed to her voice tone, which resembled the thunder sound, and became louder and louder until he cried out or pretended to be asleep. My father told me that she was extremely beautiful, which had fascinated him, but he discovered later her bad manners, the rudeness of her tongue, and her love for false pride and gossip. He disregarded her actions at first, but she went too far in her wrongdoing.

My father stopped, as usual, contemplating the ceiling for a moment. I felt his hidden tears in pain as he remembered those difficult days bitterness.

He soon started another story about places he had visited in his childhood and youth. The stories were overlapping so much that it was difficult for me to understand some of them, but they were really wonderful and entertaining.

I had never seen the sea, but he described it to me to the extent that I kept imagining this endlessly expansive water. He patted my hair and promised me to visit it, but his chronic illness had prevented this. The sea wasn't only what I didn't know, but there was much of what my father narrated about places and even characters he had known. He was elaborating sometimes so that I could go on in my imagination and that I could understand and perceive what I heard from him. He repeated some of the stories over and over, and, strangely, my fantasies were changing according to the way he narrates the story, perhaps because he was adding a description of important details at that time.

I loved his stories with all their details and accuracy until I became addicted to them more than the books he used to read to me;

he was always proud about having them in his small library, perhaps because they were real and much more alive than the stories in those books.

Those moments of happiness were disturbed by cases or waves of depression he was going through, I didn't know the cause. Sometimes I tried to get him out of his silence and sadness by inventing funny stories that were in fact taken from his real stories that he had previously told me but funnily or so I thought. His beautiful facial expressions were always reflecting my success or failure extent in what I did. A small smile meant nothing more than a compliment. As for the laughter that was accompanying the funny situations that I recount, and upon his request sometimes to retell it to him again, it was confirming my success in my mission.

Sometimes I wasn't able to retell it completely, so I had to invent new events or try to remember some of the events that I had previously made up in my previous narration; the strange thing was that my father never tried to remind me of any of my stories details while retelling them; although he had a good memory, he would let me go on even if I went into a different narration from the story he asked me to hear. It wasn't a competition between us in the art of telling stories, but it was just small exercises that a pupil did in front of his tutor to assure him of his good perseverance in his lessons.

I couldn't stop thinking about his suffering, which even though it had been so long, made him sad and depressed just remembering it; the woman he was talking about didn't look like my mother, as he has already spoken about my mother differently.

She is indeed his ex-wife, but he hadn't been able to forget her bitter actions. The sorrow couldn't be forgotten, as he always repeated. He bequeathed me his grief, or perhaps we were destined to live in permanent sorrow.

I still remember my childhood friend Haim, the only friend I saw myself in. We used to spend most of our time together in a childish play that extended until tiredness or the parents' intervention to end it.

I still remember well that day when we set up a hammock that he made of ropes, he brought from his house, and he sat on it under the blazing sun. I was swinging him and then would run to the shade because the sun was causing me burning eyes and heavy tears.

The hours in which he enjoyed sitting on his swing were so long, not caring about the strong heat of the sun. He was like a butterfly; I could hardly look at him because of the itching, which was followed by a blur in both my eyes. I wanted very much to apologize to him and go home, but he begged me to stay with him. I wouldn't remember how long we have stayed, but I never forgot those hours as long as I lived.

The next morning I knocked on his house gate, as usual, but I didn't expect to hear that news that came down on me like a thunderbolt; Haim is dead. I couldn't see him or even say goodbye. There were many questions that I asked my father, just to understand what happened to him and the secret of that brief answer from his family.

At first, I didn't understand the meaning of death until I experienced the pain of separation from Haim. I would stand for hours waiting for him to come to play together, sometimes I was imagining him coming, so I rush towards the mirage. I have suffered a lot.

I didn't understand and didn't accept this bitter fact. My father patted my hand on my shoulder, so I turned towards him firmly and hugged him for a long time and cried and cried. I would wish I had found a similar bosom the day I lost my father; it's the most difficult *loss and always renewed in my life. Even Sarah, who came with all her beauty stealthily to console me, couldn't firstly relieve me of my sadness, fear, and depression.*

I didn't remember that day how I was able to sleep, perhaps my tears, which completely dried up in my eyes, had instructed my body cells, so drowsiness had crept into them little by little. I remember that I woke up with a completely exhausted body. I spent the first week visiting his grave and inspecting his clothes and belongings, touching them and feeling them, and drowning in his good smell stored in his clothes.

My Father, My Father…

I cried more than once, but my cries faded into the widening void. I was terrified by a shadow that I thought was an illusion, and then it seemed real, so I got scared and curled up on myself.

Sarah has appeared, so my body cells laughed; she appeared with a sad smile and facial features that combined sadness with all beauty. It seemed that she heard my cries and realized what I was in and came. She sat next to me that day and swore to feed me pies of her own making.

The delicious taste of her pies made me forget my sadness for a moment; I was chewing it and enjoying its taste and Sarah's beauty. Between confirmation and denial, her sympathetic kisses had dispelled the sadness atoms that inhabited the place.

I hadn't got enough of her innocent kisses on my pale cheeks, so I touched her hand and her hair and kissed her forehead and cheek; she tried to withdraw, I begged her to stay and I clung to her more. She was trying to console me with her body and I was renewing my hot kisses, confirming my approval and affection for her. They were pleasant moments of the most enjoyable things I had lived. She allowed me to embrace her more and more, the weight of my sluggish body had hurt her, so I leaned on my four limbs. She repelled me repeatedly and embraced me repeatedly in successive childish movements that brought us to the climax of ecstasy.

She withdrew with heavy steps until she was out of my sight, and if hadn't it been for that sticky semen that forced me to change my clothes, I would have thought it was a dream and nothing more.

The long working hours helped me get out of my miserable condition. I had always dreamed of finding my father with his smile and his welcoming words when I came back home in the evening. He would dispel my fatigue and strengthen my determination with praise and encouragement words, but over time, I realized that my father's death is a fact that must be accepted.

My father warned me a lot about Sarah, I don't know what the similarities were between her and his first wife. Whenever I started talking about her or her mother, he began to recount some of his tragedies with his ex-wife. That wife who loved the others' compliments about her beauty and had gradually immersed herself in the corridors of pleasure until she became one of its pioneers. My father turned a blind eye to her actions, thinking that she was just foolishness, but she went too far until she began to openly declare her immorality and decadence and tell him what happened in her privacy with her lovers. Sometimes he had to silence her with slaps that were burdened of the daily hard job that chained his body and mind.

She liked to torment him after returning from work at the end of the day, reeling from fatigue and grief; so she would receive him with her arrogant looks and a body that hides many secrets. After a simple dinner, he would lie down in his bed hoping to enjoy some relaxation while she used to sit in the room corner, fiddling with her hair and pouring her provocative questions for him to anticipate his invitation to her to the bed. At first, she would tell him some of what she knew about men, then would touch upon the particulars that she would prepare him for so that he would accept what she would tell him later.

She was a shrewd, mischievous, and slutty woman; she was pretending that what happened between her and the other men was nothing but rape, in which she was the victim. My father told me that he often hit and kicked her to keep her silent, but she never stopped being sadistic with him, so when she ran away with her Greek lover, he accepted it as a deliverance from his misery and depression.

My father didn't tell me these details, but I read them in a letter she addressed to him, which I found after his death among his private belongings in a wooden box. I've never seen a woman like her. She could have left silently with her lover, but she chose to stab and pierce what was left of her sharp blades in the heart of my poor father through her clear and frank words about her sexual relations with other men.

Vulgar words and obscene descriptions of debauchery I didn't hear. What hell that my poor father had lived through. What aches did that weak body bear? Her letter had completed the missing links in the stories my father told me. So the events were clearly arranged in their logical order in my mind. What a fate was it that the prostitute and her pimp escape to a bigger brothel! What a fate was it for my mother to die before she sees me! What if had she survived?

She would have stayed with me after everyone had left me alone, squatting in the room corner, talking to myself like a madman after burying my father. In vain I tried to imagine her. What woman was she? Why my father did not keep any memory of her to enable me to decipher the talismans that surrounded me.

The sounds of pebbles that had fallen on the house courtyard interrupted my crowded thoughts, so I hurried to find out the matter. I stopped reading and couldn't finish what I started. I wished I knew this man more. He owned the house we live in now. I contemplated the citrus tree, his friend, in his loneliness, perhaps she would answer the many questions that accumulated in my head and occupied my mind and thinking.

I thank God that he numbered the pages of his scrolls, or I would have to get lost in its maze that looks like talismans. Indeed, his handwriting isn't beautiful, but at least it's readable.

The children's noise pulled me out of what I was in, so I hurried to prepare food for them. I tried to focus more on what I was doing because every corner of the house made me imagine that tormentor. I tasted the food several times, suspecting that I had added salt more than once during my stray.

My mother-in-law tried in vain with her repeated questions, to find out what was happened with me or to get me out of the drowsiness state that suddenly overwhelmed me. My little son's comment after eating made me laugh when he said that the food wasn't delicious as usual, except that hunger is an unbeliever, as he said, and with hunger, everything could pass.

I ate a few bites. Yes, my little son was right in what he said, so I hurried to the kitchen and prepared something delicious for my husband before he came back home.

The Exile

I hastened to open the door, for the strong and successive knocking made me shudder with fear. As soon as I answered the police officers my name, they took me with them, without I utter a word. It was strange; I tried to remember anything so that I could understand the reason for what was happening to me. Their harshness and cruelty forced me to remain silent and to walk with them even to the gallows. They kept me in a small room alone for a few days, and then they began to convey me from one person to another, one of them handed me over to another one as if I was luggage or a pet. I didn't say a word, for I know the penalty for that, even when they put me in a wooden carriage with many other loads.

We all set out in a large convoy of carriages loaded with bags. The cavalry lightness and speed that surrounded us on our path caught my attention. My tears fell as I followed the scene of my beloved city, Damascus, as we were moving away from it little by little. I would have liked to scream or ask what I had done, and where are they taking me? However, I suppressed my compulsiveness, as usual.

I swayed like the bags surrounding me right and left and began to adapt that I'm a bag like them, no more, except when someone asked when we stopped if I wanted to go to piss, so I was nodding my head positively, and meekly. I was allowed to stay away a little bit, either because of the crowd around us or because of the submissiveness that I had shown them in a somewhat wary calm.

I lowered my pants in a spot I found, which I thought might hide me from their peeping eyes, which were waiting for me to piss, and that almost killed me while we were walking. I cleaned the feces that had been stuck to my body with small stones that were around me, and then I rubbed my bare buttocks several times in the soil to make sure that all the dirt was removed from them.

We spent some time having a break, the road was very tiring. Someone threw me a loaf of bread; I ate it greedily, and I began to contemplate their movements and try to listen to their strangely overlapping conversations until the same person came back and gave me another loaf, so I embraced it and began to chew it, hoping I could dispel the harshness of loneliness and the hardship of the road.

I went back to previous events, perhaps it could explain to me what is happening; what do I have to do with them, why do they give me those strange looks? And especially that person who used to check me from time to time, and throw me a loaf of bread or a small piece of cheese. I wouldn't look at him; his eyes were frightening, checking me as much. I would quickly lower my head so that our eyes wouldn't meet and then raise it again after hearing the sound of his moving away. He has a large body with two wide shoulders, I had never seen in my life wider than them, and a terrifying hoarse voice.

We returned to the march that seemed more merciful than his looks, so I went back to think about the past. Why am I here? Where are they taking me? And what did I do to lead me like this?

My father has taught me to obey the police officers, for he would always repeat: Disobeying them is big trouble, the first of which is an insult and the last of which is impalement! One day, on our way home, my father noticed that there were a number of them in our first neighborhood, and then he pulled me by the hand, and we followed along a narrow path until we reached our house. I don't forget how my father was trembling for fear of them and avoid meeting them for any reason. Oh, my father, you bequeathed me even fear and submission.

We continued our exhausting march; I would contemplate the desolate and barren desert, that was empty except for sand and some grass scattered here and there. I contemplated the mountains far away from us while the sun was setting as if it was hiding behind them. I was fascinated by the beautiful colors that added to the place a breathtaking beauty, which I had never seen.

We stopped suddenly to rest and sleep, so the soldiers scattered to go somewhere to relieve themselves as well. I moved away from them also to empty my bladder, which was filled with urine to a painful degree. I tried to hide in a secluded place that I needed to empty my body of its waste.

Darkness had quickly descended upon us, and I hurried to join the convoy, and suddenly one of them grabbed me from behind with both hands and forcibly dropped me to my knees. I was small compared to his size, I tried to free my body and push his weight away from me, and when I realized the impossibility of that, I started screaming. He put his right palm on my mouth, while he started pressing my buttocks with his other hand, his weight started to increase, so I hit him with all my strength with my right elbow and following with successive blows from my left elbow, even my feet started fighting fiercely his body.

He started slapping me and hitting me to stop screaming, and if someone hadn't intervened in time, he might have been able to get me. He took him away from me with a murmur between them, as I was busy lifting my pants, and then I hurried to the carriage, slipping through the huge bags fearing of what happened.

I slept that night with nightmares that I couldn't get rid of for many nights, which made forgetting this difficult situation almost impossible. I woke up to the sun stings and hurried to piss near the carriage, and I was no longer safe of their brutality and treachery. I didn't pick up the loaf of bread from him as I used to, and I didn't dare to look at him even when he got away from me. I didn't expect this brutality and filth from him, for I thought he was the best of them.

O, I'm stupid! I thanked the Lord who sent those who kept him away from me and from his evil.

The hardship of the road seemed to me thousand times more merciful than having a rest with unpleasant consequences. I was trying to avoid him and his disgusting looks along the way; if I wouldn't have been in such situation, I would have spat in his face dozens of times.

The day had quickly passed, and it was time for us to have a rest; so I prepared for myself a safe place among the huge bags that surround me, fearing this reckless do it again. My guess was right and I woke up when I felt his attempt to get hold of me, but he ran away when he realized that he couldn't stop me from screaming.

The journey was getting more and more difficult, either because my strength had failed and I couldn't bear it any longer, or because I was increasingly afraid of these soldiers' rudeness and arrogance.

They were drinking tea while laughing and telling their endless stories; I have listened to them sometimes and turned my ears off from them at other times.

On the way, we have passed by a herd of sheep, so the shepherd gave them some milk and they drank it all. I wished that they would let me share it with them since I was addicted to milk, but he was punishing me and deprived me of milk, and even he has replaced the loaf of bread with a disgusting moldy loaf. Consequently, I had to eat it completely, for hunger didn't leave me another choice.

Memories had overwhelmed me, and those morning sessions in which I used to have breakfast with my father. In fact, they weren't full of delicious food, but they were the most delicious, in my opinion; the milk had an unforgettable taste with the puffier and fragile Damascene brioche. My father was giving me a second and a third piece, and, with his sweet smile, was asking me to chew it with a cup of hot milk.

Oh, I miss you, Dad. I wish your departure had been delayed a little.

The boring day had passed, for the road was the same. I waited for our break time, and rushed to find a place to relieve my body of its waste. I squatted, completely absent-minded, disturbed by constipation that began to haunt me and cause me great pain, after which I sat with my bare buttocks on the soil. I was exhausted all the time squatting in vain; when I was about to get up to lift my pants, I saw him coming quickly towards me.

I couldn't escape, as he rushed me with his cruel and merciless fist. I didn't find at that time a means to escape, except to throw at him what I had of soil in my palm, which fortunately had entered his eyes. Thus, he fell and cursed me with the dirtiest words; but I had escaped from him. I ran to the convoy seeking help to protect me from his villainy.

Nightmares came back to haunt me, and I couldn't sleep that night, not to mention the stomach ache, which made me scream and vomit everything. Finally, they sympathized with me and gathered around me trying to help me. Someone gave me dry sage leaves and I chewed them reluctantly. It was very bitter, and then I drank a glass of water and fell asleep. I started to shiver and scream until someone threw a thick blanket on me that I was in dire need. Then I went back to sleep again. The carriage continued its walk again, away from yesterday's vomit effects.

I raised my head, looking at the sky and the landforms around me, which started to differ somewhat from what I had seen before. The painful stomach cramps returned, thus I leaned against the carriage edge to vomit again. The stomach pain was accompanied by a terrible pain in my head, along with weakness that affected my entire body.

We stopped in the Bedouin regions, and it seems that someone had asked for a cure for my condition, so an old man came to me and asked curtly what happened with me and checked up my tongue and eyes. He went for a while and then came back with a cup and asked me to drink what was in it, so I did; I didn't like its taste, so I spit it and my painful vomiting came back with severe cramps in my stomach until I felt like it was going to come out of my mouth.

The man patted my shoulder and gave me the cup again to drink. I drank it reluctantly and then I went into a sudden nap, after which I woke up by the water that the man sprinkled on my face. He asked them to keep me with him, so they carried me to his tent, where he covered me with heavy blankets and gave me hot drinks of different tastes. The man took care of me and offered them to host me for a longer period, but they flatly refused, under pretext for leaving quickly from the clan's region.

I endured my pain in the carriage; I relaxed at times and straightened out my seat, exploring the road strange landforms at other times. Time had passed so slowly that I thought the time had stopped or almost would stop. I tried to listen to their conversations and their incessant laughter to understand the reason, but I failed in that.

We were in our room, so he noticed that I was busy reading these scrolls from time to time; he asked me about them, and it seemed that he meant my question to him when he was alone with me. I told him that they were autobiographical sheets, thus he added that he didn't expect I would like them to this extent and that he almost threw them with the rest of the other items outside the house, but the pottery jar aesthetics in which they were preserved made him abandon that.

The discussion between us didn't last long, as his long fingertips have quickly crept in the darkness into my body, groping and pressing it. I had thought that his desire, which was renewed after we had alone a private room, would fade with time. I was completely wrong, as he was surprising me with his growing desire. I let his hands infiltrate deeply and intimately all over my body, yielding to the delicious numbness that hastened to permeate all his body cells.

He woke me up before dawn with his hot kisses as he used to do. I knew he would do what he did last night. We were still naked and his semen was still in my body, but he didn't care for that and went on with hot and quick kisses all over my body from my lips to my toes, which used to intertwine with his toes from moment to moment. He didn't foreplay me for a long time, and yet we had a very good time. Our morning intercourse had a completely different taste from the evening one. I would have liked to be together naked under the quilt so that my skin might rub his rough and hairy skin, but he quickly withdrew to get dressed in a hurry. Despite he seems daring while being naked, but as soon as he puts on his clothes, returns to his usual shyness and hurries to take a bath.

It didn't take a long time to have a bath; he quickly urged me to hurry to have a bath before his parents woke up...So I did.

The scrolls were calling for me to continue reading them, but I put them off until I prepared breakfast and finished my daily work at home. I had finished everything and I was very happy. My husband Fahd's wonderful touch left a good impression and a renewed joy that gave me what I needed to quickly accomplish my duties and go back to pick up those scrolls that had become my obsession and curiosity to know the rest of the events.

I started imagining him from what I read about. A handsome, somewhat introverted young man is dating his neighbor girlfriend, who seemed to be more passionate about her, away from her mother's looks, who was stalking him, trying to keep him away from her daughter in various ways and tricks.

But why was she doing that? I asked myself.

Why does she hate him? Where do they take him? What is his fault? And what did he do?

My youngest son's cries took me out of my questions, as he was tired of his brothers' disregard, so he jumped into my bosom, as always, and I hugged him and patted his head and shoulder while he surrounded me with his little hands and then fell asleep.

I leaned my head against the wall while embracing my little son and my head was filled with questions. I was curious about what these scrolls would have contained future events.

Deir Ezzor

We have arrived at dusk. But where am I? We penetrated the narrow paths to huge doors that lead us to a courtyard that leads to a large number of small rooms. They were peeping at me while they were busy with their affairs. I was a little apprehensive about that until they took me to a small room to sleep in alone. I didn't say anything, perhaps tomorrow would explain what was happening to me.

In the morning they took me to an officer with sharp features and scary looks. He told me that I was forcibly expelled from Damascus and that I had to spend my life here in Deir Ezzor if I wanted to continue alive. It was the first time I heard that name! He asked me if I understood what he said. As soon as I answered negatively, I received a strong slap from the soldier accompanying me according to the officer's order. He repeated the previous sentence with the same question, and asked me if I understood his words, I answered: Yes, of course.

It was a clear lesson to acquiescence. Everyone laughed after he allowed me to leave. They took me to a gate that led to a narrow path that seemed to me like a maze.

I don't know how? Where do I go? I walked a lot until I passed the houses to the surrounding orchards. I had nothing to eat, thus I ate fruits from the trees as much as I could.

I was so tired, so I fell asleep under a huge tree until I was awakened by the successive pokes of an old peasant's stick. He asked me what I'm doing in his orchard, and when I told him my story, he sympathized with my tears that accompanied my explanation to him of what I was in. The man hosted me in his house and served me food.

I didn't need to eat as much as I needed to understand the truth of what was happening to me. What did I do to be alienated from my home, and my city, Damascus? The oppression had reached its apogee, so I stuttered in my conversation with him with a painful rattle and pain. Perhaps fate led me to this man to relieve me of what I'm in. His children flocked to him shortly after, they were more than I expected, and some of them were close in age. I knew that he was married to four women and that his wives were racing to have more children, so I laughed at the sarcastic manner he uttered.

He liked kidding, although his facial features didn't seem that. I didn't quite understand their accent, especially when they were talking to each other. Some of the vocabulary seemed strange to me that I hadn't heard before. The amplification of the character (Q) and (J) was evident in their accent, to the extent that they would invert the (Q) to (J) strangely and vaguely. On the third day evening of my stay with them, he offered me a cup of tea with a strong taste and started talking about himself and went a little further, explaining to me some of his questions about me.

I understood that, so I briefly narrated to him my life course... It was necessary to address that secret that I had previously hidden, so I uttered it at once. He remained calm and listened to me, but his eyes bulged out with obvious astonishment. I tried to explain to him more, but he apologized for not completing our session, for he has to wake up early to go to work in the morning.

His withdrawal was a nice notice from him that I should leave his house, and he surprised me in the morning with sustenance he gave me when I was about to leave, wishing me a successful journey. I said goodbye to him with a worried smile, while I was thinking where I have to go, and what will happen to me? I made my way back to the narrow and winding paths.

I was tired of marching as I walk and walk. I stopped from time to time and looked around, and asked myself what am I doing here? In the end, I found a hallway that led me to a closed church, with a narrow corridor adjacent to it; I approached it very carefully, to rest my tired body by lying down on the soil and sleeping as it was. I woke up the next day to an old priest murmurs. He was surprised by my presence, and then he brought me a wooden chair and invited me to sit. He was asking me very cautiously and my answers were honest and slow. Then he asked me if I would like to be introduced to a Jew who lives near the church. I immediately answered affirmatively. The priest escorted me to that Jew, who welcomed us, and he explained everything to him, and then he said goodbye to me and left.

The man listened to the priest after he had left work on a wooden carpet-knitting machine in a small room next to his house. He greeted me and introduced himself as "Ezra." He invited me to sit down and went about his chore with the sounds of the loom wooden bars that were working in harmony. I sat and surveyed the poor room in the middle of which was the carpet-knitting machine "the loom"; it was an old wooden machine, with a sofa that had been put next to it, apparently for customers. Ezra noticed my presence again, so he asked my permission, and returned with a plate and a loaf of bread, which he put in front of me, and went back to work behind the loom. I ate the loaf and tasted the yogurt topped with rich cream that refreshed me with its magical taste. It was a thick and crunchy cream, which forced me to cut a bigger piece of bread to dip more of it.

I didn't care that he was peeping at me, for I was hungry, and the delicious cream forced me to eat greedily.

Do you want more? He asked me after seeing the plate empty, and I answered him negatively. Finally, I had a strange feeling of comfort and reassurance, especially with his constant smile on his face. I told him about myself and the reason for my presence with him, but he didn't answer anything. A friendly and caring smile, followed by a laugh was enough for him, he said: I also came here against my will. I was eager to hear his story, so I knew that he had been traveling between Deir Ezzor and Aleppo for a long time, selling some products to the Bedouins, and then he soon became familiar with the place and settled in it. I saw that his hair had grown long, so I asked him to cut it. He hesitated at first, but he agreed after I assured him of my experience in this field.

He lowered his head after he gave me scissors that were next to him, and I went to trim the white hairs that were very long for him. He relaxed completely and almost fell asleep, but suddenly someone came in and greeted him in a hoarse voice.

He welcomed the man who offered him a quantity of ghee and they agreed on a fair price. Ezra took the ghee bowl to his house and showed the man a beautiful rug that he had just finished making. The man bought it at once, and he would pay the rest of the price next time. The man went joyously with his new merchandise, and so was Ezra, happy with his lucrative swap, and I came back to finish his haircut.

He used to ask me to assist him with simple things at first, and then had gradually increased. I didn't know if he needed all these things or if he took advantage of my presence and asked me for them. I fixed his house rooftop with a mixture of straw and mud as he asked me. I mixed it with my bare feet and carried it on my back disregarding the old wooden ladder that was swaying under my feet, and then I spread it with another layer which pleased Ezra with the splendor of my mastery when he saw it. He patted my shoulder and offered me a special delicious food that suited the hardship of what I had done.

Ezra was clear with me from the beginning that he was in need for someone to assist him and he wouldn't skimp on paying what he owed. I had no other choice, as the man offered me a room adjacent to his house to sleep in with what I needed from food in return for assisting him with everything he asked me for.

I started getting used to the strange environment of this area and getting to know its secrets through its many customers. I learned from him commercial bargaining, as he was a veteran of buying and selling despite the simplicity of the materials he bartered.

I woke up to screaming and wailing that had terrified me. The sound was strong and interfering, I didn't recognize it well; I thought it was a nightmare, but it was real. A man I don't know well has died. Maybe I had seen him by chance several times. His house was adjacent to Ezra's house, but its gate overlooks the other street. His body was brought out at noon for burial.

I remembered my father's coffin and remembered that fateful day. I had previously asked him about death for I was afraid of it. On that day, he avoided responding, and with time he told me about that event to which we will all go obediently. He told me at that time about the day of his mother and father's death, and how the last moments were. Only then I understood that death means a forced and eternal absence.

I asked him while I looked into his eyes: Will you die too?

He replied: Of course.

That day we exchanged silent and despondent looks and for the first time, I felt that I didn't want to understand his answer... It was a big maze. I hugged him for as long as I could to belie his honest answer. Some facts aren't only painful but complex talismans. I read a lot about it and tried to understand that thing called "Death". I wanted to understand that feeling that I'm getting from time to time, it isn't pain or premonitions, it's a strange and unknown condition.

The sadness in this small town was also strange, with different rituals from what I had known, as the females wailing escalated from time to time with collective crying, wailing, and successive rattles. When the coffin came out of their house, I saw the women slapping their chests and scratching their faces with their nails, while sadness overwhelmed the whole place. My eyes had filled with tears; I remembered all my sorrows at once. I approached their home during mourning time to hear those melodious voices lamenting the man's virtues with a unique and successive tone with the other's mourning.

I was attracted by the strange situation, so I followed it. Everything here was different from what I had known of sadness and environment. There was a huge river and sprawling orchards on its sides, followed by the desert with Bedouin life.

Now I realized Uncle Ezra's secret attraction to this environment in which urban, rural, and nomadic life had intermingled, which resulted from daily swaps that simply secured his livelihood.

I brought the lime as requested and went up to the rooftop to cover it with an additional layer that protects and preserves it. Uncle Ezra was busy with his work when his daughter went out to survey the commotion I had unintentionally made, so I immediately apologized and she laughed too. Her beautiful face forced me to apologize more than once so that I could have another few minutes, stealing as many looks as I could for this angelic face, which I couldn't forget in the following days.

Ezra had praised my work and I had received from him a bonus and appreciation; a bonus that began successively to increase with every new work he assigned to me until I became his right arm. With time, he became more and more dependent on me, and I, in turn, worked hard to please him. On our way to get dates, he asked about my opinion of finding a house for me to live in, and I agreed with him. He informed me that there are two rooms, one of which I will use, and the other in which we will store some goods coming from Aleppo and Baghdad.

One day, while we were drinking tea together he asked me if I wanted to get married, so I answered him immediately: Of course. Nonetheless, he didn't complete the topic but cut short his speech by referring to the work that we'll be carried out on the next day. That night I thought for a long time how I would propose to marry his daughter without causing him any embarrassment. I found nothing but grumbling about the loneliness and the difficulty of carrying out my home affairs alone, but Uncle Ezra was only smiling and patting my shoulder as he murmured: God is generous. God is generous.

I could no longer stand his repeated response, so one day I surprised him with my intention to search for a wife for me; his mysterious smile irritated me, and I repeated my words. Thus, he finally said that he wanted me as a husband to his daughter, therefore I agreed immediately.

Uncle Ezra and his wife had prepared everything and it was the wedding day! Uncle Ezra took me into the room where my wife was standing in the corner by the bed, and she had completely hidden her face.

He asked us to repeat what he would say so that we would be blessed. Then he went out wishing us a happy marriage. I approached her with longing and wanted to stick to her, so she turned away from me at first, and with my repeated attempts she sat on the bed, so I sat next to her and she revealed her face.

I didn't discern her well in the dark, a darkness that our shyness forced us to like. I kissed her, and she turned her face a little, and I couldn't be more patient, so I held her head between my hands and kissed her on her lips. She surrendered to my insistence, so I proceeded to sip her lips and touching her white body. She tried to get away from me several times as I got closer and closer to her. I enjoyed her wonderful body, which gave me various kinds of pleasure until I surrendered to the weakness that engulfed my body. I ecstatically lay down on my back and I could hardly believe what I was in.

I woke up the next day on the door-knocking. It was Uncle Ezra; we exchanged greetings in short words, I looked down at the ground, as I was ashamed of him. I took from him a basket covered with white cloth. I thanked him and he left in a hurry. I didn't find out what was in the basket, but I rushed to my bride to embrace her again. She expressed some displeasure with my erotica, but I didn't care. I began to find out her face as she was avoiding looking at me, she looked a little different from what I had seen before. She covered her body and face again, while my body was in a struggle to stick to her and make love with her again.

We spent a wonderful day together enjoying ecstasy with the delicious food presented to us. Uncle Ezra didn't give me more than two days off, and then he asked me to hurry to assist him in the work. When I got home, her mother and her sister were at ours; oh my God!!! it was she who I saw her that day!

I looked at her and couldn't believe what I saw! Their visit didn't last long, but it left me with gloom and astonishment. I spent the rest of the day finding out my wife's facial features and listening to her voice. Oh my God, how didn't I notice that? Perhaps it was because of the similarity between them. Lust had overcome me again, but she disregarded me; therefore I took off my clothes, and stuck to her despite her resentment.

I didn't care about her apathy, but when I tried to kiss her, she turned her face away from me, which has pissed me off. I hid my angry and approached her again; my body was greatly raging with lust. She tried to get away and hurried to leave the room, but I pulled her towards me violently; thus, she fell to the ground and started shivering and the foam was coming out of her mouth. I didn't know what to do...I raised her head and shoulder, but she started to shake with successive shivers. I tried to splash her face with some water, but she didn't wake up, so I rushed to her family and informed them of the matter, and we all returned to her, praying to God for her recovery.

She slept in the other room while her mother remained beside her, taking care of her. It was a difficult and strange day, and I fell asleep that night with a reproachful conscience. She seemed tired and weak, but my lust overcame me. I wished if I would have stopped.

A few days later, Uncle Ezra brought an old woman, hoping that she would heal her with herbs. When I was alone with her, she didn't look at me; I felt inside her a hatred that I didn't understand. Otherwise, when I tried to embrace her, she started screaming, as if I was about to rape her, so I left her alone and slept in the room corner. All my attempts to get close to her were in vain as if revulsion had worn her from head to toe.

Uncle Ezra asked me to allow her to stay in their house for some time after he explained to me that her illness had returned after he thought that she had been completely cured. Therefore, I began to adjust again to the forced celibacy life and occupy myself more and more with work.

At this time, Sheikh Ibrahim had visited us, asking Uncle Ezra to make a rug for him. It was the second time I saw him so I sat next to him to listen to his interesting talk. Uncle Ezra told him about my proficiency in haircut, so he asked me to cut his hair, and when I finished he thanked me with the kindness that I was accustomed to from him.

Uncle Ezra informed me of his intention to take my wife with him to Aleppo to treat her because her health condition was deteriorating, and her epileptic seizures had increased to a frightening and alarming degree. Consequently, the whole family had traveled, but Uncle Ezra has returned after a long time alone. His youngest daughter (my former love) got married in Aleppo, and my wife stayed with her mother in their grandfather's house because she needed a long time to recover from her illness. I felt his estrangement and his treatment has changed, and he began to work to dispense with me, so as soon as Sheikh Ibrahim offered me to help his relative in his shop because of his old age, I agreed immediately.

I said goodbye to Uncle Ezra, who in turn said goodbye to me with a lukewarmness which I wasn't accustomed to, even though I terminated my marital relationship with his daughter according to the terms he had dictated to me and upon his request.

Now, when I look back on those events, I don't know who was wrong about the other. He had admitted to me that she was sick, and had hidden it from me, and I only had a normal marital relationship. I thought it was reluctance and shyness no more. I rarely saw Ezra anymore, and we both started to avoid each other.

My thinking pattern has quickly converged with Sheikh Ibrahim, so when he told me his intention to travel to Damascus, I suggested to him to stay at my house, so he thanked me and said goodbye with gratitude. I knew that he had many acquaintances in Damascus. I would have liked to ask him to help me to go back to Damascus, as my heart had melted for it, but I waited for the right time for my request.

His relative was older than I expected and boasted of his expertise in herbal medicine and cupping besides his work as a barber. Sheikh Ibrahim returned from his trip to Damascus, bringing with him the Damascene gifts that I had missed. He told me a lot about its beauty, so I felt that I had been absent from it for decades. I took this opportunity to tell him about my problem and my strong desire to return to it. He didn't mind and even he expressed his willingness to help me.

Sheikh Ibrahim had inquired of a friend of his here in Deir Ezzor about my problem, and he told him that the solution of this matter is exclusively from Damascus and that my stay in Deir Ezzor depends on that. The news of Sheikh Ibrahim gave me hope, especially after he promised me that he would ask again for help from his acquaintances in Damascus to find a solution to my problem. Cupping was done for him as he requested, so I began to look at the dark blood drops that were sprouting from his shoulders. Then I remembered my father when he was sitting one day, just like Sheikh Ibrahim, and his blood drops settled in the small glass cups.

Oh, how I miss you, Dad. I wish you would visit me. I wish I would make you cupping to relieve you of the blood that bothers you. I wish I could touch your prominent and tired back vertebrae. Oh, father, how much I longed for our walk in the narrow alleys together and talk together.

My feet led me to Uncle Ezra; I didn't forget his favor with me. I stopped at his small workshop door. He was resting his head on the wall, so I muttered in a low voice, and then he noticed me and looked at me silently. Thus, I hurried and kissed his hands and he hugged me with both of them. I couldn't speak and my tears fell profusely, so he sat me next to him and wiped his tears and mine. I told him: I wish I had died, but that this would happen, I had never intended to hurt her, it was a passing affection between a husband and wife, I thought she was joking with me, so I pulled her towards me and she fell, I wish my hand had broken before that.

He said while patting my head: You don't have to, you don't have to, it is Lord's will, and this is fate and destiny. We thought she was cured, so we didn't tell you about her illness, and I found in you the son-in-law that I wished for, and I didn't want you to marry the younger, as that would negatively affect the eldest. I loved her very much, she suffered a lot from this disease and its psychological effects on her, and we didn't hesitate to visit whoever doctor we heard about, so we thought she was cured. I love you but that's better for all of us. Her health condition is in severe deterioration, and I should stay with them in Aleppo. I have returned to collect my debts and will leave for Aleppo soon.

He had offered me to rent his house, which was better than that in which I live, so I thanked him for his kindness. I said goodbye to him and I was very satisfied. I did well by coming to say goodbye, I would have blamed myself if he had left without apologizing to him.

On my way to visit Sheikh Ibrahim, I passed by the city center, and I wished if I hadn't seen a hanging man. I didn't get very close to him, as the place was crowded with pedestrians, and the crowd murmurs that surrounded the execution platform had increased. He was apparently in the prime of life, so I quickly went away, I couldn't handle what was happening. They took me before and exiled me here without guilt, so how if they pay attention to my looks against them. I had avoided hearing what was said about the existence of traitors to the Sublime Ottoman State who had been liquidated from time to time. My father told me that he used to see the gallows in Istanbul to punish those traitors. He told me: The most difficult thing is seeing them on the impalement for several days, with blood dripping from their bodies.

When I met Sheikh Ibrahim, he was tired and didn't explain the reason. I cut short my visit to him after I finished his haircut. From there I passed by a shaded tree which I used to sit under it and hear the Euphrates River rustling. We were like friends, he and I. Our conversations were indeed almost silent, but they were beautiful and expressive. Sometimes the Euphrates voice rose and sometimes the wind blew, so the branches would start dancing. I was sharing their jokes with successive sneezes or a sudden cough.

Ezra had kept his promise to me about his house and even had left some of his things to me free of charge, and after my insistence, he accepted a simple piece of gold, I begged him to hand it to his daughter. He folded it into a burgundy cloth and hid it in his huge belt. He added sadly: She needed more the Lord's care. Several days had passed before my final move to Ezra's home. His customers had begun to come with their loads to barter them, just as he had used to do.

Hannah

I have heard from my customers what was being said among the public about the riots spread in the Upper Island, which made me more careful in my movements. I have bought a mule to carry on it the goods I had bought from Baghdad and Aleppo, even though I wished in my deep heart to do what Ezra had done and to go back to my city, Damascus if I could that.

This was the only time I had envied Ezra, how much I wished I could have the freedom to go back to my home in Damascus. A woman named Hannah has visited me and reminded me of herself; she was Ezra's neighbor in Aleppo. She's also a resident of Bahsita, the neighborhood that Ezra always told me about.

She looked beautiful and bold and used to wrap her cloak in a way that made her body charms appearing sexier; she has needed my money and I have needed her body more, and that was always my losing trade. She was a chatty woman, as soon as she became alone with me during her periodic visits; she was pouring all kinds of news into my ears.

She got used to my silence when I hear what she tells me until she realized that sometimes I deaf my ears in my manner, so she used to repeat to me this tragic news many times. Perhaps she repeated it out loud to get me out of the silence and gloomy I was in. She was surprised by my weeping when she informed me of my ex-wife's death, Ezra's daughter. She embraced me to console me, but I moved away from her a little, wishing to be alone because I wanted to weep for a very long time.

She realized that, so she embraced me and kissed me again. I surrendered to her because I know very well the extent of her determination to reach her goal. Little by little, my oppressed body was getting high with her deep and magical touches until all my limbs shivered at once. I don't know what this woman's secret was, as soon as she turned away from me, I promised myself not to repeat that, but I soon surrendered to her erotic touch.

She was many years older than me, she didn't reveal her real age, but her body folds had exposed it. Sometimes she was trying to appear it through her extensive tenderness and other times, she was leaning coquettishly like a girl who had just realized her first menstruation. I didn't care too much about her psychological fluctuations and her gossip, to the extent that I didn't pay much attention to her sneaking out of the house.

I had hated my weakness in front of her, which had forced me to accept her with all her inconvenience and bullying. That weakness brought me to where I'm. When we did it together for the first time, she used to be the one to start and the one to end. I got angry at myself when I saw it oppressed, even with a prostitute who had practiced prostitution with a bunch of rabbles. I didn't say anything even with her false actions, as she was the one who decided when and how, and I had to completely obey her. She had caught me imagining her as my beloved Sarah. This malicious doesn't miss anything, even she got into my imagination by force. Otherwise, I must admit that I needed her, for I'm alone in a completely alien environment. I didn't expect it would be so harsh and dry.

I was often interrupted by quarrels that lead to bloody punches, such as the fight of cocks, which I heard about. I tried to avoid everything that might get me into trouble as much as possible, even the ant on the road I would pass over for fear of smashing it, but the most important reason was my longing to return to Damascus so that nothing would stand in front of my return to it. Despite my father told me that we aren't of its original inhabitants, as my grandfather came from Alexandria, but in his youth, he was associated with a strong friendship with a young Samaritan, and when he invited him once to visit him at Mount Gerizim, he gladly accepted the invitation and stayed with him for some time.

However, his joy upon his return clashed with the rumors circulating against him about his converting to the Samaritan religion, despite his categorical denial of that, and his bad relationship with the rabbi Joshua had led to problems that troubled him throughout his life. This was the situation that imposed on my father and me the solitude that we had become accustomed to with the time.

I never thought of staying in Deir Ezzor despite the improvement of my financial condition to a large extent. The daily swaps, despite their small profits, had secured me a good income due to their large number. Ezra had used to satisfy his customers and I had treated them the same with a smile and kindness as well. Sometimes I was boring for long arguments and bargaining with them and tried to shorten it, but my awareness of their nature and their tendency to gossip forced me to accept their rudeness. The successful business begins and ends with a smile, as Ezra used to say.

The number of shops had increased with the increase in demand and the expansion of trade with the Bedouins, Aleppo, Baghdad, and Mardin. Deir Ezzor was the cross point for everyone, in which the deals of commodities were exchanged from one party to another. From Baghdad had come dates and grains, and from the desert had come the sheep and cheese, while Aleppo was the most important source of oils, spices, nuts, and tea. And if it wasn't that Hannah had withdrawn my full pockets, I would be a huge store owner. She was sharing my profits by force...

I didn't sleep all night, my mother-in-law tried to reassure me, but I was very afraid. She had assured me that she took it away from him immediately. I was cleaning the house courtyard when I heard her screaming, so I rushed to her to find out that she was carrying my baby in her hands, and she said that he had been stung by a scorpion. My husband rushed him to the hospital, while my mother-in-law struck the dead scorpion again for the tenth time, and her angriness wasn't relieved until she burned him while she was reciting some of the Qur'an verses. It was a difficult time followed by more difficult hours until my husband sent us news that the baby had improved.

After they returned home, my mother-in-law had prayed to thank God, and she delighted us with a dessert she made especially for him. She was feeding him with her hand while she was looking at him, and her eyes dripping with joy. I knew very well her love for my children, but on that day she was a different person. She sat him in her bosom, kissing him and reading the Qur'an verses. In the following days, we got occupied by checking the house walls and floor, and when my father-in-law, Abu Fahd discovered a hole in the wall that we hadn't noticed before, he immediately closed it tightly.

The Flood

I was woken up by the fast, strong successive knocks on the door; I thought that I was dreaming. I rushed to open it to be surprised by a crowd of people and their screams came about speeches I didn't understand at first, so they forced me to get out of the house. Then, I knew from them, about the Euphrates flood!

We spent a night in the open air on a small hillside and we remained in our panic until we knew its waters had receded, and then we returned to our home. Our neighborhood was in a better condition than the neighborhoods adjacent to the rivers, which were badly damaged, and some houses were completely destroyed. I saw the other side of my dear friend Euphrates, whom I always thought was beautiful, and he's like that, except that his anger is really frightening.

Here, the population's magnanimity and kindness had appeared in their solidarity and sympathy for each other. Sometimes I feel that we need strong crises to keep our souls away from hatred and wrath. I was saddened by the drowning of a girl who was about to get married. Their old house was stormed by the terrifying flood, and the river carried her away. Most of the houses were filled with sadness, which has increased Deir Ezzor's miserable atmosphere. Hannah has been away from me for a few weeks, but she came back with a wonderful surprise. Delicious food, she advised me to hurry up to eat it while it was warm, so I did, and although I hadn't tasted that type of food before, I loved it. A simple but delicious dish, I was refreshed by the ghee smell that permeated the place, so I ate it greedily.

It's a special dish of this region called "fora or kishka"[11], with dried and boiled green beans, and some spices, that I don't know, had given it a wonderful taste. Some additions, even small ones, could change even the whole thing. In Damascus, we used to eat kishka with onions and dried mint with small pieces of bread, and here the addition of boiled green beans had giving it another taste. I wished Hannah would stay for a while to hear my praise for her cooking, but she always comes so suddenly and leaves in a hurry.

Sheikh Ibrahim came in with his usual smile, while I was busy devouring the rest of the "fora". I greeted him and apologized for not being able to provide a similar meal. He had a books collection in his hand bag; he gave me one of them, wishing me an enjoyable reading, so I thanked him. Reading was the comfort that takes me to other worlds that I hadn't seen before.

Sheikh Ibrahim had used to provide us with books. I knew that others were waiting for him impatiently like me, so he said goodbye and left in a hurry. Sheikh Ibrahim wasn't an ordinary Sheikh, but a human encyclopedia; in addition to that he wasn't fanatical like Sheikhs' majority whose visions were confined to a specific framework. I don't know the reason that pushed him to include me in his group, which he became its literary and cultural sponsor, but through it, I have satiated my passion for reading. My joining of Sheikh Ibrahim's group was limited only to the books and manuscripts that he offers, as they had other activities of private evening's sessions and seminars.

During her visit, Hannah had informed me of her desire to return to Aleppo. She said that she could no longer tolerate the police officers' rudeness and harshness. I got annoyed for her sudden decision, despite her secret visits to me and her annoying gossip, but she was the happiness window that dispels my depression and pain.

---

[11] Translator: a mixture of soaked bulgur in yogurt, and then dried and grounded.

Sheikh Ibrahim had also informed me of his intention to travel to Damascus for a private matter. I didn't ask him about the reason, but I wished him a safe return. Before he left, he brought me a large number of important books. Sheikh Ibrahim bade farewell to my thoughts and feelings, and on the same day, my body bade farewell to Hannah, who would come to spend a special time together.

On that day, she cooked "mash'hamiyah"[12] that delicious specialty meal of Deir Ezzor to increase my body elasticity and my lips softness, as she said. She made me laugh with her insolent and endless debauchery. Although she claimed that she had repented of the prostitution she had practiced in her youth, the slips of her tongue and her daring comments soon exposed her. She had left, and I was patient that I would get used to loneliness again.

Fear had returned to dominate everyone, with hanging some people on the gallows bars, and even several others were impaled. I had heard it but hadn't seen it, and I was astonished by those who go especially to see it. I confined my day to work and reading, and I began to avoid talking or even commenting on the news circulated by some about the looting that has recently increased, in addition to more decrees of the Sublime Porte[13]. I received an excellent Aleppo gift from Hannah, who sent it especially for me with an Iraqi merchant named Ezekiel. I thanked him and offered to host him, but he apologized for being busy with many things that he had to accomplish in a hurry. He promised me a soon visit upon my insistence on hosting him.

I got confused, so I paid attention to these scrolls' arrangement until I organized them all in the correct order. I noticed my mother-in-law's smile, and she was looking at me while I was passionately talking to myself, so I smiled at her despite my knowledge of the truth. My husband interrupted us with some sporadic news about what was happening in Palestine. As usual, my mother-in-law dropped dozens of curses on the Jews and the English.

---

[12] Translator: tandoori bread kneaded with minced fatty meat and herbs.
[13] Translator: Ottoman Government.

I quickly prepared food for them; I know how much my husband loves this dish despite its simplicity, so I make sure to prepare it from time to time. "Eggplant Mutabaq"[14] is a nice and easy dish, and most importantly, everyone loves it. Only my father-in-law sometimes has complained about his stomach after eating it, so I sometimes add potatoes and green peppers to it. I had the utmost respect for this man, and my memory only preserved the positive scenes about him. Despite his simplicity and spontaneity, he had the utmost magnanimity and generosity positions. He treated me from the beginning as his daughter, and I loved to be as he wished. My children had inherited from me his love, so they were racing to win his love and satisfaction.

My father told me one day about a comrade named Kislev, whom he had met in Istanbul. He had many good memories of him, but he only told me a few of them. I could imagine this man, who befriended my father for some time. It became clear to me more why I was called by this strange name, the meaning of which I was often asked about. Kislev was a potter who, with his creative hands, could form beautiful pots from clay. I don't know what brought them together? Perhaps, it was the alienation harshness in that big city, and perhaps was for many reasons that I wasn't not aware of. Kislev had a sense of humor, even in the most difficult circumstances, which my father had needed with the difficulty of his life and the harsh living conditions.

I sometimes imagined them walking together in Istanbul squares or on the Bosphorus sides, one of them singing and the other humming, to forget the alienation gloom that was awaiting them from time to time. I don't think he was a normal person for him, I realized this, from his face's secrets of when he talked about him, and he was a friend who later would miss him all his life.

It seemed to be a hard and gloomy day because of "Al-Ajaj"[15], this annoying guest who blocked out the sunlight until it was completely dark. I had never seen such a wind, saturated with sand and

---

[14] Translator: cooked spicy rice topped with fried eggplant and meat.
[15] Translator: a desert storm laden with sand and blocking the sun's rays.

dust, with its frightening sound and its mighty power. I could hardly shut the old wooden door in its face, and hurriedly entered my house, for the winds laden with dust threw off their load at once, and the stranger than this, their colors which differ from time to time, sometimes dark red like blood and sometimes dark brown.

I moistened a piece of cloth with water to wipe my face with it and inhaled the air through it because this difficult weather had suffocated me. I had had these nagging fits before, that day I was busy with my work with Ezra, and we didn't notice it until a dusty wind hit us, so Ezra hurried to shut the door tightly, and when he saw it, I couldn't breathe easily; he hurried and washed my face and gave me a piece of wet cloth from which I could breathe and after that, I felt better.

I was amazed at the public's chant after that, "A hundred times dusty are better than one time snowy." The fact is that each people have a certain way of thinking that we may not understand. I thought it was due perhaps to the incursion of this area into the desert away from Damascus and Aleppo, and perhaps for other reasons that I'm not aware of.

Is it reasonable to compare the smoky wind with its dust and sand with the snow in its innocent pure white color, and the good it carries for nature and man? The strangest thing is that I have seen some people who not only bear the name of "Ajaj", but they also named their children by animals' names or ridiculous funny names. Ezra had told me that, and had warned me against being sarcastic or even laughter at what I heard from them. They are characterized by warm-blooded, so you may see a person laughing happily, but suddenly he changes his mood and becomes angry and cruel, and perhaps he stuck his dagger into his interlocutor's body in the blink of an eye if he heard what he didn't like.

Ezekiel has kept his promise, and came to visit me; I hosted him for several days, most of which he spent on his trade, which was his main preoccupation. I asked him about the books he had, and he told me that they were his only comfort in his many travels. When he knew my passion for reading also, he gave me one of them as a gift; I thanked him a lot. Before his journey, we went together and shopped for some gifts that I would like to send with him to Hannah and Ezra. I said goodbye and wished him a nice journey.

Abu Sultan had visited me with his thick and coarse hair, he sat on the wooden chair as usual and started telling his stories. I listened to him sometimes and was busy with his hair density at other times, for he was hairy to a strange degree so that it was difficult to distinguish the end of his head hair from his neck hair. The annoying thing is that he was very stingy and leaves his hair long until it reaches an unbearable degree, which forces him to come to cut it.

He would notice that I was busy with my work, so he would recount the story he had started so I could pay attention to him and listen to it. Truth be told, some of them were so funny that made me forget some of my fatigue. I have often needed a nap after the trouble of cutting Abu Sultan's hair, so I used to get relaxed in my seat and recalled some of his strange stories.

Suddenly I remembered the book that Ezekiel had given me, so I took it out, and took advantage of my free time to read it, although its beginning was normal, I began to yearn to finish it. I was happy for Sheikh Ibrahim's return and met him at a dinner at one of his followers, who was also one of my customers, and he invited me to the feast in honor of Sheikh Ibrahim. I accepted the invitation with some hesitation. He greeted me with his wonderful smile and seated me next to him; I was overjoyed, while everyone was racing to carry the huge "Mansaf"[16] and put it in front of him. The pieces of meat have crowded in front of me, and Sheikh Ibrahim did it also, and the others have successively raced to put the meat also in front of me, to the extent that we all laughed spontaneously. The dinner was very delicious. It consisted of Saj bread[17] dipped in a meat soup and original ghee with goat meat grilled on hot coals.

---

[16] Translator: a huge plate of cooked rice topped with lamb or goat meat and served with yogurt.
[17] Translator: griddle bread.

Their way of eating was rather strange, as one of them was very skilled and formed a small roll of meat and bread with three fingers and then ate it quickly. I was eating slowly, and I thanked God that one of the guests had the same problem; otherwise I would have been embarrassed if I had stayed alone at the table.

We stopped eating after our stomachs were filled with food, and then they brought us tea to speed up the digestion process according to their opinion and customs. It was a brewed tea that I've got so addicted to it; I think the boiling water over charcoal was the secret to this wonderful flavor. It was a wonderful day, I spent it eating and listening to jokes, some of which had surprised me, especially in Sheikh Ibrahim's attendance, who was smiling to encourage his pupils to go on with this.

It became clear to me for the first time that Sheikh Ibrahim hates the Turks through his pupils' sarcastic comments about police officers as well as his implicit comment against them. I went back to my house reminiscing about the wonderful moments of that beautiful evening that had pleased me, and I wish it would have happened again.

I was laughing when someone was repeating the sentence he had said by Deir Ezzor's dialect in Standard Arabic so that I could understand it, they realized this when they noticed that I wasn't responding with them. How much I wished I was like them laughing without reservation or fear. I peeked at them while they were performing a group prayer behind Sheikh Ibrahim, who surprised me after sitting with a sentence that made me laugh. He told me: The matter is easier for you, but for Abu George, it is more difficult.

I didn't understand at first, but he clarified what he meant that I am circumcised like Muslims. Then, I forcibly had laughed. It took me a long time and I was joyful to relive those wonderful moments from time to time. My joy didn't last long, as I had severe diarrhea that made me spend most of my time moving between the toilet and my bed, and I had drunk herbs that I kept for such a state until I felt that my intestines would get out of my body. Perhaps because of the large amount of fatty food I ate, as I had never eaten such large quantities as the ones I had eaten at this feast.

He lay down next to me thinking that I was sleeping, so he turned his back to me and slept on his side. It caught my attention that he was absent-minded throughout the day. I didn't ask him, so as not to draw his parents' attention, but I kept checking his movements. I got closer to him and my leg started touching his leg, he didn't care so I kept getting closer to him and I let my thigh touching with his thigh. He suddenly noticed and looked at me, so I pretended to sleep and stuck to him more. I could feel his body warmness and my love for him. He noticed again my constant touching with him, so he turned and kissed me and our eyes had met, but he misunderstood them. I was hoping he would tell me what he was feeling, but he quickly took off his underpants to have sex with me. He thought what I did was a desire to have sex with him, but I was just hoping to hug his head to take his worries off his shoulders.

His body was upping and downing until became combined with my body. I opened my thighs more and was completely absent-minded. He continued his penetration, but he was also absent-minded like me, but with what? I don't know!

A few moments had passed before he lay down on his right side, he was still close to me, and so I turned. I wished to embrace him, but the silence was the situation's master, even that sound accompanying the friction of our bodies was also muffled. It took a long time and we were still close, attached to the body, and separated in mind. I was obsessed with what he had hidden in his silence and closed in on himself. I noticed his quick withdraw from my body as the last drops of semen flowed down my thigh. The darkness surrounding us had concealed what we were in. I didn't know how he managed to reach the ecstasy. He turned his back to me and a few moments, I heard the sound of his snoring. I also turned my back to him and soon fell into a deep sleep like him.

I was surprised by the presence of many priests in Sheikh Ibrahim's house when I visited him. He welcomed me and introduced me to them. I knew that they were from Mardin. They were very reserved, so I opted to withdraw from their meeting, and went to the river to relieve myself a little. I was absent-minded, remembering what had passed, when a fisherman interrupted me, showing me the fish he had caught. I refused to buy them, so he offered them at a lower price and so on several times until I was ashamed and bought them. The price was so cheap; it looked like he was in dire need of the money. I took them and went back to my house talking to myself about what I would do with them because I'm not a good cooker. I wished if Hannah was here, she would have made of them a delicious plate.

I thank God that he washed them well with the river water; otherwise it would have been more difficult for me. I remembered what Ezra usually was doing, so I brought the barbecue tools and put the fish on in several batches. Soon the smell of barbecue spread all over the place. I rushed to Sheikh Ibrahim to gift him the largest part of them, and I also did with some of the neighbors who had sent me some of their food in the past. Finally, I sat enjoying the taste of the fish tender slices.

I remembered my father when he had prepared fish one day and we ate it together. Ah, that different flavor. My father was keen at first to take out the thistle completely before putting it in my mouth, and then he would chew his bite again and start telling me different stories about the mermaids and the magic lantern. My father was keen to make me eat with his right hand while telling me his masterpieces. How many were the stories wonderful when they were accompanied by delicious meals!!!

Sometimes, I wished I belonged to this region, with its advantages and disadvantages. In the morning, I go out like them to my work, and then meet with my relatives and friends. When I got home, I wished I belong to anything. I wished I was a Damascene, a Muslim, a Christian, or a Jew. Unfortunately, I wasn't any of that! I wasn't Damascene, that's how I felt with their looks at me. I wasn't a Jew despite my formal affiliation; they accepted me as a follower of this religion but it was a reprehensible matter at the same time after it was spread that my grandfather has converted to the Samaritan religion in addition to his disagreement with the rabbi.

I didn't know? What was my fault in a dispute that I wasn't a party to and didn't even witness! What was it my father's fault that he spent his life alone? Perhaps if we were rich, the matter would have been completely different, but rather everyone would have hastened to gain our friendship and our affection. Sometimes I feel alienated here, but when I remembered my alienation in Damascus, I found that the situation wasn't better, as some have monitored me and have tired me with their hatred.

I was amazed at my eternal love for Sarah, and my eternal hatred for her mother. He lied who said, "Like mother like daughter." No, this isn't true at all, so how the roses could be compared with the bramble? I went away with my imagination while I remembered her. She was my first love. I didn't remember when I saw her for the first time. We were kids playing together in the narrow alley of our neighborhood, but I remember getting more and more attached to her over time.

She might have upset me once or more, but I couldn't stand her anger, so I was quickly apologizing to her and reconciling her. She was so beautiful and I was happy to be close to her. How much I'm now miserable being away from her!!! At first, she didn't pay much attention to me, but when she realized how much I love and care about her, she released her feelings with a wonderful shyness. She wasn't like me. She had friends who would visit her and play together in her house. I used to peep on them from our house rooftop until my father saw me once and rebuked me, but I kept peeping without his knowledge.

Oh! Dad, I wish you were still there, I wish we were still together, chatting for a long time until you fell asleep. One day her mother was talking to her friend about something, I didn't mean to eavesdrop, but I felt that she was talking about us and I was a little surprised. However, the cat, with his sudden voice, drew their attention to me, so I got stuck of fear in my place. She rushed to *complain about me to my father, who was forced to slap me to please her. Her voice rose while she was talking to him, and she didn't get calm until she heard his strong slap sound on my face.*

I didn't see my father sad as I had seen him after that, although I apologized to him and kissed him, he repeated his warning to me of my actions' consequences. I admitted I was wrong in what I did, and I couldn't control myself. I wished that she had agreed to listen to me to explain the matter to her. Nonetheless, it wasn't easy for a woman like her to listen. Her sharp and stern facial features had blocked the way for any goodwill gesture towards her.

My husband brought me a bundle of white papers; there were many things to write about. I began to summarize what I read and add on another page scattered words that will come together one day to form useful sentences or perhaps a story. My husband didn't disclose to me what was wrong with him, and I didn't ask him, so I entrusted the task to my mother-in-law. She knows how to question him when he keeps his silence. At tea time, my husband told us that the UNRWA might force us to share the house with another family. My father-in-law has muttered vague words in response to what he heard. The next day, my father-in-law insisted on accompanying my husband to go to the UNRWA's delegate and to explain our situation and the distress we are in. Before he left, my father-in-law has repeated what he would say to the delegate, by explaining the matter in front of my mother-in-law, as if she has the absolute solution. He fell silent after she told him that he had to remember and say it verbatim to the delegate, so he got aware of himself and kept silent.

They didn't inform us of their visit result to the delegate, so it seemed that deciding on the matter needs some time. During the following days, my father-in-law didn't stop repeating phrases about the house's narrowness and our large number, and he almost talked to himself repeatedly in the house courtyard. I could hardly stop myself from laughing when I saw him moving his hands and angrily defending his opinion, talking to himself away from our eyes. My father-in-law had insisted on my husband that he should visit one of their acquaintances, to explain the matter to him, and ask him for help to solve this dilemma. They did well, because this visit has shown later, that it had contributed to keeping the situation as it is. Therefore, my father-in-law has restored his happiness, enjoying a cup of tea beside the small trees he had recently planted.

Hannah had surprised me with an unexpected visit, and I knew from her that she had come to collect some of Ezra's previous debts owed by some of his customers, and I also learned that she may turn to the police officers because Ezra couldn't be able to collect it before. Of course, she didn't tell me their tacit agreement, but there was certainly a common interest that they will share with the police officers in return for collecting almost non-existent debts. She waited for several days, and she then returned to Aleppo with her friends. I said anxiously goodbye to her because of the words she said to me. She asked me to be careful in everything, for the information she had, confirmed to me that many things will happen soon and may result in many tragedies.

She insisted on repeating that to me many times, so I became sure of her information and her concerns credibility. She had already advised me to collect my debts and to be ready for every emergency that may happen. Nonetheless, the sentence that I didn't understand was that I may see many bodies hanging from the gallows or being stood on the impalements. She asked me what I know about Sheikh Ibrahim. I didn't want to tell her anything, so I talked about the generalities of what I know, and I prayed to God in my heart that things would turn out fine. I was terrified by the coincidence of her question about Sheikh Ibrahim with her talk about the gallows and the impalements. I wished I hadn't seen her; she made me worry about what she said. I became like a madman, and the thoughts took me in a long way. Her words weren't random and she wasn't of the kind who throws it lightly. Surely there is something I don't know.

Of course, what she knew was also known by Yuzbashi Jamal[18] , as she was like a ring on his finger and she knew almost everything from him. Hannah always carries out Yuzbashi Jamal's orders

---

[18] Translator: ottoman military rank means captain.

immediately and without thinking, as she wasn't only from his entourage, but from his followers who used to be submissive to him without thinking. If she wasn't being like that, I might have told her and had asked for her advice. Sometimes we have to hide some things even from those close to us, either for the privacy of the matter or the other's nature. I remembered a tale I had read, how a sentence or even a word uttered by someone had taken his life. I was indeed in the prime of life, but what I had lived through and my father's insistence on the necessity to keep silent had made me think carefully before answering any question.

I was able to control my tongue, and I had perfectly managed it. As for that thing hidden in my pants, I couldn't tighten its bridle; as soon as it saw her he would rebel against me and make his own decisions. She was indeed the one who attracted him to her, but he also got used to her, so he followed her submissively as she wanted. I didn't rule out that she told Yuzbashi Jamal about our secret relationship, for his look at me and his facial expressions make me feel naked in front of him. Therefore, I was keen to stay away from him while she was keen to kneel at his feet. This was that has scared me of her, so I had kept my secrets away from her, and she was aware of that with her innate intelligence. She had tried to penetrate my mind through him, and unfortunately, he quickly responded to her and got erected with respect and appreciation.

Nonetheless, I was careful when he was entering her corridors that she might enter through it into my depths, and with difficulty, I was taking him back after a great effort. She was skilled in everything, a dark and frightening cave, despite the pleasure she gives me. We have to admit that not everything we have is really ours, even if it seems like that; a follower could become his master's opponent or his enemy's door.

Sheikh Ibrahim had traveled secretly to Damascus; he had entrusted only me with that. I wished he could postpone the trip for a while. If Yuzbashi Jamal might ask me about Sheikh Ibrahim, I might answer him that he's one of my customers. Yes, he's a customer, no more. As for the books that he had given to me, it's his nature. He's *like this with everyone. He didn't single me out for that, but some were closer to him than me, some he had taught them to read and write, and some were sharing the praying with him and others had attended his meetings. Why do I care about his private affairs? He had rented my house in Damascus and gave me all the due rent. It was true that on his last trip he had entrusted his secret to me, but I know nothing else. He wanted to travel secretly to Damascus, and if I wouldn't have been the house landlord in which he might stay, he wouldn't have told me. Why do I care about with his meetings? I had never participated in them, and I was accidentally invited, but I had my preservations and they had theirs as well. I'm not one of them. They didn't want me to join them, it was just mutual compliments. Why am I guilty of what I didn't commit?*

I woke up to the nightmares that were haunting me a lot. I was afraid of tomorrow, I used to take refuge in my house after every new news I hear about the erected gallows to hang the Sultanate's enemies on them.

I had read a manuscript on herbal medicine, of course, I had some information; my father told me about it, and we kept some of it for medicine, especially thyme, sage, anise, and many others. I think most homes in Damascus were doing this, but I had found in this book much more information than I know. I had read the book with great eagerness for reading, and reread it, to the point that I had memorized it by heart. I have asked my customers to bring some herbs that grow far from the river. I had never seen a town with such variation as Deir Ezzor, even the taste of its river water was so different that its vegetables were better and richer in taste. The special atmosphere of that area had helped me to dry quickly the herbs, some of which I had brought during my wanderings outside the town and kept them in wicker baskets and paper bags that I had specially prepared for that.

I didn't intend to do skewer ironing for any of my customers, but against his insistence, I did it for the first time. At first, I was hesitant and afraid, but later I found it very simple. They were few stings of a red-flamed skewer. The sight of the skewer after I had removed it from the hot coals had scared me, so I hastened to place it on his naked body. He had felt a weakness that began to creep into his left hand, so he flinched at first, but when I found him determined, I continued it with successive stings.

That was my first practical application of what I had read. My work in herbal medicine[19] was well received and encouraged by others. Sometimes I used to treat them with "cotton ashes," for in some cases, it was the only cure. I put cotton ashes or something similar to the desired place and its surroundings several times. I hate pain and blood, but fate wanted me to do it against my will. I couldn't treat some of the pus caused by the deep and old wounds of a young man, so I advised his family to take him to Sheikh Saeed's clan, but they insisted that I have to accompany them, and it was a wonderful day.

We went out to the desert, where the wilderness in all its forms and spaciousness. In a spacious tent, Sheikh Saeed has greeted us with his smiley face. They have served us a sumptuous Bedouin breakfast, and all of us had eaten. The old woman began to treat the sick young man. She was an old woman whose reputation had widespread in treating patients all over the region. I have assisted her with my experience, and she has praised what I had done for him. It has required more than one day, so we stayed another day in their hospitality. I liked their way of spinning the wool and their beautifully woven knitting before our eyes. Everyone was smiling, and the happiness had pervaded the entire spectacle, unlike what I was accustomed to in Deir Ezzor, as gallows weren't there from time to time and nobodies had been hanged without knowing the reasons. The women hurriedly have prepared a large "Mansaf" with the Saj bread, meat, and broth. We ate with great appetite, especially after we felt the signs of our patient's recovery.

I don't know whether the woman has accepted the reward that the patient's family has offered to her or not because they argued about that far from our hearing. We came back around the afternoon, and I sat next to him in the wooden carriage, following up on his condition and checking on him. When we arrived home, his family has paid me

---

[19] Translator: alternative medicine.

so generously. He was a wealthy and generous family's son, and Sheikh Ibrahim had previously praised them for me, so I made sure to dedicate myself to helping them. I went back to read carefully the book, as there were some herbs that I didn't fully understand, although I have asked the Bedouins about them when I visited them, and they gave me some of what they have had, but there were still many of them that I hadn't found yet.

Yuzbashi Jamal

On my routine visit to Yuzbashi Jamal's office, it had caught my attention unusual procedures that warned of something. Of course, I couldn't find out, so I thought to leave it until tomorrow, as he might disclose it to me. I have brought some money to give to him, but he has surprised me that he wanted to do cupping, which I didn't expect. He usually asks me to cut his hair, so I always bring my tools with me. His soldiers were always disturbing me, for as soon as I would leave him after I cut his hair, they came to me with the same request; I was hastily doing so that their number wouldn't increase, or I might have to spend the rest of the day in their forced hospitality. He got angry when he heard my excuse, so he called his soldier to bring me what I wanted, and he quickly took off the upper part cloth, sat on his chair, and turned his back to me.

At first, I have massaged his back with oil so that I could easily pull the cups up and down. I have tried to control myself from the fear that might run through my body as I have lit the wick, put it in the cup, and stuck it to his back, and then pulled it off, causing red spots. I saw his comfort, so I suggested to him that we postpone the phlebotomy for the next time and suffice to draw the air from his back, so he has agreed.

I have needed some time to be able to stop my hand shake when touching his naked body, especially when I have seen his reaction when the wick has touched his skin. I thanked God that he had turned his back on me and didn't see it, I don't know if he has felt it or not.

He has let out dozens of groans afterward, I didn't suffice only with his back, but I continued to his shoulders, his both hands, and his neck.

It seemed to me that he was needed to relax more than cupping, so I massaged his scalp well after using a little oil, which made it easier for my fingertips to work perfectly. He didn't praise my work, neither had thanked me. I found myself compelled to tell him that I couldn't do that to his soldiers; so I asked him to tell them about this and not to distress me with their impossible requests when I come out, so he had giggled and agreed. I wished I hadn't done this massage for his scalp, for he got used to it that he has forcibly added it to his weekly program. I wished I have only done cupping him that day and hadn't added anything else to it, for he was used to giving orders and giggle for a long time.

After a while, I have suggested to him to perform him cupping because it doesn't take a long time; so the cupping wounds might also force him not to ask for anything else until he is completely healed; consequently, it will cause him unbearable pain. He has accepted, without knowing my real intention; my hand is no longer trembled like before, he has bowed his head in front of me with his flabby fatty and strange body.

I have phlebotomized the gathered blood which had fallen profusely at first and then slowed down little by little. I did many scarifications on his body with my sharp scalpel, enjoying for the first time the sight of his blood drops settling in the bottle. They were thick and disgusting. This man has told me from the beginning of my arrival here that my neck is in his hand, and that he can crush me in one moment like an insect. His threats were repeated in every forced encounter in front of him.

At that time I had goosebumps all over my body. I was so happy to see him leaning his chin on the back of his chair, bowing his head, surrendering, and flexing his arms peacefully. I couldn't count the wounds that I had done on his flabby body, as I was keen to cover his entire back; I anointed his back with oil, and I wished in my mind *to use salt or vinegar or even lemon so that he would spend his day groaning and writhing from the severity of the pain. I helped him to get on his clothes while he was reminding me of his kindness with me, so I nodded my head agreeing with his words.*

One day, he asked me about an herb that I could recommend to him. It was a disguised request, but it was quite clear to me. On my next visit, I brought him the appropriate mixture. He has informed me later that he liked it, and asked me for more and of course, with an ugly and annoying laugh. I wished if one day he would complain about his liver, so I may prescribe to him to drink wormwood and bitter melon even if by force. Indeed, I wished he would drink it.

I knew a lot about him, as Hannah had previously told me his secrets; he was who brought them to work in forced prostitution. They were the pleasure tools that he had used to hunt others and increase his grip on the city. Everyone had feared him, for he was the gateway of happiness and misery at the same time. He knew everything about them through his spies and eyes that he had planted everywhere, so everyone has submitted to his might. We were forced to share with him our profits as a partner, sharing our profits equally and perhaps more. As for the girls, they were his maids and slaves; they were living in the brothel that he had prepared for them to practice prostitution with the men and rob them of their money and minds as well.

They had to tell everything that has happened to them to the pimp, Zeina, who would extract from them what might interest him, and pass it on to him. He might listen to her and seek more clarification. Sometimes the mystery was surrounding some men, so they were luring them again, but by other girls who were more experienced with the men's secrets, to sip everything from them, and then to tell it to Zeina to explain the picture to Yuzbashi Jamal later.

All of them were completely naked in front of him; so if someone may brag about himself and tried to show his strength in front of a crowd, as soon as he may hear Yuzbashi Jamal's voice, he would remember his real level; and then, he may hasten politely to denying his previous talk, and shut up immediately. He made people think that their livelihood and their public and secret pleasures are in his hand, and he could swing them on the gallows or sit them on the impalement. People were whispering and secretly circulating those terrifying stories about him.

Hannah was his first victim, and then she has moved with her good obedience and submission to him to a better rank, and through her success in the delicate and difficult tasks he had entrusted to her, she had been able to capture his admiration. I had heard him repeating this sentence many times: "If Hannah wouldn't have been dear to me, she would be somewhere else."

I might understand what he has meant, but I didn't understand the reason for repeating this sentence. I have surely understood it, and completely complied with him. He has wanted to include me in his special entourage, and I was afraid of that. Hannah had previously offered this to me, but I have used various arguments. Her advice was that we are weak in the midst of crowds that had imposed on us a secret dependency to rely on in adversity. As for me, I had a different point of view, which was completely similar to my father and grandfather's path through self-distancing.

Each one of us has a philosophy; this is how life varies with the diversity of our skin, tongues, and thoughts. I went home and fell into a deep sleep. In the morning I have reviewed the manuscript again and studied it well and knew that I was needed some herbs to complete my mixture.

The next day, I went to the market and searched for the herb that was still missing at a farmer who has used to sell the plants he brought from the other side of the river. The man laughed when I told him that the herbs found in the east of the river were different from those in the west, and he replied:

-Because they are from two different environments and that is why they were called by different names, "Al-Shamiya and Al-Jazeera."[20]

He followed while he was sitting on the ground and while I was busy examining his goods: "This is from God's grace upon us."

He also told me as he put his Shemagh[21] back to his head: "The needs are the strangest." I didn't understand his brief words, so he sat down to explain to me that in Deir Ezzor there was another environment, which is "Al-Howaija", meaning the island that sits in the middle of the river. Nonetheless, he said, warning me: "But the snakes and the scorpions wouldn't let you see anything."

---

[20] Translator: the Levantine and the Island.
[21] Translator: white cover cloth for man head.

Maria

Yuzbashi Jamal has summoned me and I was surprised to find Hannah accompanying him and I knew from her that she had returned upon his orders and he asked me to escort her to an important matter. They had a sick girl and he wanted me to treat her secretly. She was very young and was a small size as well, and I don't know how she could tolerate such work because of her small body. I don't know who has suggested to Yuzbashi Jamal to convey her to my house to take care of her until she would recover. He had issued his orders, and I have submissively carried it out without any discussion.

She had frequent convulsions, so I warmed her and prepared for her an herbal infusion hoping that it might cure her, but she has vomited with an unpleasant smell. I tried to control myself, as I almost vomited because of the disgusting scene; the poor girl was ashamed and lowered her head. Hannah has saved the situation by her visit. She wiped off the vomit, changed the quilt, and threw it out of the room. She took out a bottle that was hidden in her clothes folds and asked the girl to drink it; after a few minutes, she asked her to drink more of it, and then she fell asleep as the children.

I don't know if her body suddenly became flabby or so I saw it when I woke up the next day while she was sleeping naked next to me. Hannah wished we could spend more time together, but the presence of our unexpected guest has forced her to satisfy one-third of her desires. She left me preoccupied to prepare for them what I had of food, and then she started telling me the girl's story.

She was a Ukrainian girl named "Maria" who was forcibly brought here, but because of the road hardship, she has suffered what has happened to her during the difficult journey with others. While Hannah went to check on Maria again I have enjoyed the scene of the cats that were having sex on the rooftop. The cat female was moaning in pain, as the cat male bent over her, clutching her neck with his fangs because she was small in size and he was huge. Minutes had passed and I was expecting them to fall together from the wall to the ground. Hannah stood next to me, watching the scene that has aroused us. I grabbed her by the hand and took her into my room. She knelt with her back to me, just like a cat, so I lifted her, and I stroked her neck, imitating exactly what the cat had done. I was aroused, and it seemed that Hannah wanted to do something she would keep in her memory to recall in the fall of her life moments, which will soon knock on her doors.

We had a great time, I rode her, and she also did by her turn the same. She had tried to do anything to make me think that we are close in age. She showered me with kisses with her delicate lips, while her face wrinkles, her prominent varicose, and her body flabbiness had surprised me with questions that I had kept out of my mind so as not to spoil what we were in.

Her experience in the body corridors had restored the youth and the sedition that she had lacked. I confessed to her that I'm passionate about her kisses, so my words and my body stabs had increased her blood flow. She adjusted her seat and got up with full vitality, to check on Maria, who was asleep. Nonetheless, she quickly came back to spread in my body again the desire for a new round that assured her of her youth.

However, the strong knocks on the gate had postponed that for a later date. It was the peasant Hameed, who came upon a previous appointment between us, which I had completely forgotten. Hameed and I went looking for medicinal herbs in Al- Howaija, so we boarded a small ship that brought us to our destination. The island was really scary and big. After seeing a snake, Hameed said: Didn't I tell you that it is full of snakes? We tried to get as far away from the thick trees as *possible, and we spent some time in our arduous search, and then we turned back when we found it impossible to go any further.*

I came back tired. Hannah had prepared Deir Ezzor's kibbeh[22] for me, which she said was different from another kibbeh. In fact, it was different. Our guest didn't eat it, but rather has sipped a hot soup that Hannah had prepared especially for her. I checked her face, it didn't seem that she had fully recovered but I think she has improved a little. I checked the bottle that Hannah had brought. I immediately yelled, "araq[23]!!!". She laughed and added: The Russians' medicine is only the alcohol. I didn't ask her where she has got it from; this weird woman always surprises me with strange things.

Finally, Ezekiel has arrived and spent with me several nights resting from the travel weariness. Hannah told me that Yuzbashi Jamal had given her the Ukrainian Maria and she asked me to take care of her until she comes back from her travel. I said goodbye to her and I was wondering by her response to my question, that she has gone upon Yuzbashi's orders. This woman was a mystery shrouded in a deep mystery, for her dark corridors lead to another, deeper and darker corridors as well.

I woke up to Maria's many movements, the poor girl. She had diarrhea because of the food that Hannah had prepared for her before she left. She went several times to the toilet. I also ate from that food that Hannah advised us. She told us that it is a popular Old Russian recipe based on cooking garlic, wheat, and milk. In fact, I didn't like it much, so I didn't eat more of it. The taste of garlic was sharp and repulsive, and it dominated the food. Hannah said that garlic is the secret of its importance; and it's a medicine for the body's weakness and sickness. I tried to help Maria at first, but I was ashamed to utter anything as I heard the fart sounds coming out of her. I now know why she didn't eat from it and she used her travel as an argument. Ah from

---

[22] Translator: a mixture of meat and bulgur stuffed with minced meat, onions and nuts.

[23] Translator: a Mediterranean alcoholic drink extracted from anise, without color, and becomes white when adding water.

you, Hannah. What did you do to the poor girl? She couldn't even lie down in her bed as she spent the night back and forth to the toilet.

I checked on her in the morning, she was sleeping so deeply; I didn't want to wake her up. I left beside her a glass of milk and a loaf of bread, for she became so skinny and looked like a ghost made of skin and bone. On my return, I brought her "Baleela"[24] and sat watching her picking chickpeas like children and eating them with appetite.

Her body was needed food, so I was keen to give her a lot of it. She thanked me with a beautiful smile that expanded more than usual because of the skinniness that had afflicted her. She seemed very gentle and silent most of the time. I wished to ask her how she got here, but I had remembered my condition, as I also came here against my will.

I spent my time preparing food and taking care of my sick mother-in-law. I couldn't read anything. My father-in-law had also lain down lazily in front of her, as he always quickly sensed illness. I offered her a cup of sage infusion with my sincere prayers for her speedy recovery. My mother-in-law's illness was often mild because she's of the type that she doesn't like those others would take care of her. However, my father-in-law was very weak in front of the illness and he complains and moans a lot.

I collected the thoughts I have read. It seemed to me an integrated story, but it needs to be rewritten again, rather the priority is that I re-read it again after its arrangement. They are indeed numbered, but their arrangement sometimes seems to be different from what it should have been.

My mother-in-law thanked me for the cup of sage and said: I don't know why the sage herb reminded me of Palestine. I smiled at her to relieve her of that pain and groan that always accompanies her pronunciation of Palestine: Oh, my God, it's the country of bounty; the country of olives, thyme, and oranges. I hope God would punish

---

[24] Translator: boiled chickpeas.

who had caused expelling us from it. My father-in-law added: Amen, Amen. My mother-in-law had also repeated it several times.

My mother-in-law continued saying: Alas, I couldn't feel their tastes, there were different.

My father-in-law replied: Don't remind me of the sorrows, my heart is hurting me, let's see when we'll return as they promised us. I'm afraid, that they wouldn't keep their promise to us.

- Let it to God, this country had been always full of wars and death.

-Ah, for Adam's sons, God had created them to build the world, but they were only satisfied with killing and destroying.

I tried to withdraw after they started to recall their old memories that I had completely memorized, and I got tired of hearing them; so they realized that and let me join in their dialogue. I poured another cup for each of them, prayed to God that it would flow through their bodies quickly and recover, so I went to those scrolls and read them more carefully. There were many questions that I had after reading some vague sentences, as well as I don't know the landforms of the area he was talking about. I'll try to read more books to find out more and understand these many texts.

I followed with my looks Maria's slow steps while she had leaned against the wall as she walked. I offered to assist her, but she disregarded me and continued walking without answering me. In the evening the vomiting has returned, but it was mild and without pain. In the morning, she was better off. I offered her the herbal mixture, but she refused to drink it. She didn't like its bitter taste; she asked for tea so I served it to her. I brought a wet cloth and started massaging her hands, she didn't object, so I continued massaging her entire body. I used a second piece of cloth after I soaked it in hot water to use it after. I lifted her arm to wash her armpits and used my other hand to clean them.

I don't know if it was laziness that has afflicted her body, or if she was so tired. I brought soap to wash her armpits, for the hair there has grown out and looked repellent and annoying. I left her in her panty and wiped her legs and feet. Her eyes had withered, so she reminded me of what I went through on the way here, crossing the desert maze. I gave her some pieces of bread dipped in milk while she had lay down, following my hand movements like a small child. Then, I wiped the milk drops that had leaked from her mouth and stuck on her lips, and then I left her to fall asleep like children again.

The incoming news had got worse day by day, and the problem in this city was, that the rumors had been made up from unknown sources. The most important was, that fear had completely dominated the people, with the apprehension of what would happen in the future. I had enjoyed watching Maria regaining more her vitality and activity day by day. She started eating everything without vomiting or diarrhea. I had hoped that Hannah wouldn't return quickly so that Maria would stay with me more, because she still needed my care, but if she recovered, she'll take her with her to Aleppo or the Yuzbashi may exchange her for something else. I knew Hannah, for she quickly might find the solutions that suited her.

Maria was in the house courtyard enjoying the small bushes scene. I stood beside her and hold her arm, but she has quickly pulled it out of my hand with childlike shyness. I brought her tea with bread and pieces of cheese, as she was hungry, so she ate them greedily.

I went out to my usual work while she remained locked down in the house. In the afternoon, I came back with what I had bought from the market. We ate together, and I peeped at her at the same time. The blood started running well in her veins, and her face became pink. I didn't know whether it was a delusion or real, I found her looking like Sarah, with her eyes and lips. I didn't notice that before. She was getting more and more beautiful day by day. I kept stealing as many looks at her as I could until she caught me in the flagrante delicto, and she became more careful in her movements than before.

She didn't know speaking Arabic well, so sometimes we got to use sign language to communicate with each other. I brought her small green apples from Al-Howaiqa orchards. She was surprised by their sour taste, and her face has wrinkled in a laughing manner. It seems that it was the first time she has tasted sour apples. We laughed together at her reaction to the point that she almost spit it out, but she got used to it later. My dear, this is how Deir Ezzor is, the city of wonders...

I couldn't stop myself from kissing her when I saw in her face my dear Sarah's features. She moved away from me, so I tried to kiss her again, but she rose and shrank shyly. I went to my room feeling the obsequiousness of what I had done. Hannah's absence didn't last long, she has returned to take her deposit. Maria had fully recovered from her illness, I had hoped to keep her with me for a while. Hannah told me that she is in need of her. She drove her while I had got pity of her. I hoped to believe her when she swore to me that she might keep her, but I know very well that our difficult circumstances make promises sometimes gone with the wind.

Before her departure, Hannah didn't forget to warn me to be careful and self-distancing of anything and not to trust those who might come from Mardin, Diyarbakir, and Nusaybin. Her words had frightened me, as they indicated a true knowledge of the course of things, and she added that I have to obey blindly Yuzbashi Jamal to ensure my safety. Her last advice made me laugh. I was about to answer her: Could I do otherwise?

Sheikh Ibrahim had been absent for a long time, and there was no news about him. When I tried to find out any news about him, someone has advised me not to do to, because no one might dare. Life had returned to its monotony, and the public had started to circulate news of sudden looting or hanging the bodies on the gallows. Fear had also become a normal thing, and it had escalated more and more, abhorrent and haunting us like our shadow. I was in my house when I have heard a strange shout and clamor. I didn't realize it at first, but the voices had started getting louder and louder. I opened the door and saw the women and children crowds; I hurried and closed the door until someone knocked on it. I was surprised by the officer telling me that Yuzbashi Jamal has summoned me.

I went with them quickly to find out the news, and I saw on our way a large crowd in the city center in a manner that hadn't accustomed to before. There were crowds of people with shriveled bodies that looked as if the ghosts had suddenly crept in them. The Yuzbashi was in his spacious office with a number of the city's notables' men, and the sounds of their discussion had become so louder. When he saw me he nodded to one of them, it seemed that there was a pre-arranged agreement between them. He told me that I should take a woman and her two daughters to my house and take care of them, so I complied with his orders as usual.

The mother had embraced her two terrified daughters in great terror. The Yuzbashi shouted at me before I left, threatening me with severe punishment if I didn't do enough to take care of them. I didn't realize it that day; otherwise, I couldn't have been able to control myself from laughing.

I tried to calm the woman, who was babbling incomprehensible words, and then she began to vomit everything, while her two daughters had continued crying loudly. I gave her water, but she has also vomited, and the same happened when I gave her a mixture of herb infusion. I remembered the bottle that Hannah had brought, so I hurried to get it and served her a small glass mixed with water, and she drank it. She recognized it immediately, for it has a special smell. She sipped the rest of the cup very slowly, and then she embraced her two daughters and fell asleep.

I couldn't sleep that night and couldn't understand what I saw at all. The successive memories had come back to me, whom I used to recall from time to time, and these new and strange facts had been accumulated with them.

The next day came and explained to me what had happened. These women had walked hundreds of kilometers in a wasteland with another group of women, and they had fallen one after the other. At first, there were some men with them, but they were eliminated on the way. Death has become a regular ritual for them; some victims were buried while others remained in the open air as food for wild beasts. Many families and villages were completely exterminated; this was what the people secretly had transmitted among themselves. Hannah was right in her warning, for the days were getting more difficult, and with the increase in taxes, extreme poverty has become a common feature.

The customers' toll has decreased dramatically, and the number of materials coming from Aleppo and Iraq had decreased because of the large number of looting actions as well. I used to complain about cutting the policemen's hair and shaving their beards, but now I thank God that I may pick up some little crumbs to subsist on it. I began to spend most of my time in my shop, leaving the Armenian woman and her two daughters freely to use the room I had given them, while I was occasionally checking on them. They were very exhausted and in dire need of rest for a long time, with their skinny bodies, sunken eyes, and wandering looks.

The youngest daughter made me laugh after I gave her the loaf of bread that I had returned with, after a hard- working day. She quickly ate it along with her sister and mother. I left them and went back to my room to read one of the books that Ezekiel had given me last time. That was my only solace, with which I got out of the absurd state that has begun to plague everyone in the city. The tales of "One Thousand and One Nights", with all their oddities, couldn't get me out of the images that have ingrained in my memory on my way to work.

There were hundreds of women; some of them were half-naked, sleeping in the streets, hungry and lost. The hardship of living has extended its wings completely to us in the homes and alleys, except for the police officers who had closed the doors on themselves and had grasped the country bounties. They had got bread, ghee, and honey while everyone outside was starving.

I have seen them with my own eyes, it was true that I have peeped at them, but what I saw was weird. It was another world behind the deaf walls, their loud laughter has bothered me and I mute my anger against their barbaric actions. On my way back, I passed by Sheikh Ibrahim's house, for I heard of their difficult situation. I had several loaves of bread in my handbag, so I knocked on the door and gave them one of them. Then, I remembered that it might be not enough for them, so I gave them another one. His youngest daughter took it from me and thanked me. I would have given them all the loaves if the Armenian lady and her two daughters hadn't been in my hospitality.

Where are you, Sheikh Ibrahim? How much do I need you now? As soon as I remembered Hannah's warnings, I would mute my conversation to myself. Fear has reigned over the entire city, which began to sink into misery and hunger, and the looting actions and sudden raids from time to time have added to it, loneliness and terror.

After he adjusted his seat, Yuzbashi Jamal asked me about Sheikh Ibrahim. I was ready for such a question, and I answered him immediately: He was only one of my customers. He laughed and said: Only!!! There was a suspicious look in his eyes, which he cut short by asking me when it was the last time I had seen him! I replied that I didn't remember because it didn't concern me too much. When I went out he ordered the soldier to give me more loaves for the Armenian woman and her two daughters. I wished that he might have given me the same to Sheikh Ibrahim's family, as they were also starving, and they were of their victims' one. I thanked him and quickly got out.

On my way back, I tried not to draw attention when I knocked on the wooden door of the grieving family. It was the second time that they didn't open the door for me, and I didn't hear any sound coming from inside. I didn't stand for a long time, for their spies were many, and I had to stay far from their evils. As usual, the Armenian youngest daughter welcomed me with her childish caress, as this orphan made me forgot about what I was in. I gave her their livelihood and went to my room after I closed their door behind me.

I woke up to the knocking on the door of my room, the Armenian woman was pleading with me, as her daughter's temperature was high. I tried to lower her with cold water compresses, but she kept shivering and had vomited everything. We all have stayed next to her; her mother was crying as she saw her daughter wither in her arms. I gave her to drink a hot herbal infusion that I had prepared for her. Then, I went to sleep, as I was very tired from working all day at the police department. My sleep didn't last long, as I soon heard the cries of the Armenian mother. I rushed to them; her body was lying down as if she was sleeping. I didn't believe that she had died until I carried her in my arms. The youngest girl was looking in amazement and strangeness at us.

The neighbors had helped us to bury her in the open area next to the Muslim cemetery. I couldn't control myself that day, so I have cried sadly and painfully. I felt that all the sorrows had gathered in my heart at once so that the bereaved mother began to lessen on me despite her great affliction.

The sad days were difficult and very bitter. I slept there alone in my shop, leaving the house to many Armenian women who have gathered there to console the mother and lessen her suffering. I missed the youngest girl, so I went to play with her; her eyes have told me that new dawn must rise one day, to dispel injustice and darkness to infinity.

I cried when they finally left my house, I wished they had stayed longer, but a friend of theirs, and upon Yuzbashi Jamal's orders, came to take them to Aleppo, where they had relatives there. I won't forget the little girl's eyes, as she followed me until she stumbled, and I won't forget her when she laughed at herself because of that. I had also chased her with my eyes and my heart had almost screamed, to beg them to stay. The melancholy had loomed over the house, that melancholy the city was forced into. The birds had no longer whispered to each other as they used to; they also left far away, even the river was running slowly as if it was embezzled its actions. The reading only had got me out of the pains which squeezed my fragile body. I hoped to return to Damascus, as I could no longer bear to live here.

The swarms of locusts had attacked us to eliminate the little that remained of our livelihood, "as if misfortunes refuse to come singly." People went out to hunt this reckless beast. The men had boiled locusts in large pots that were usually used to boil wheat. They had thrown hundreds of locusts into hot water, some of them tried to fly and escape, but the hands rushed to bring them down to join and die with their species. We all ate locusts as if we were taking revenge on them for what they had done to us. The situation was tragic, as they eliminated all the crops relentlessly.

The taste became delicious; I didn't accept it at first because of their appearance, but hunger had forced me to eat it one by one. The remained boiled locusts were spread on the rooftops to dry them and then store them; everyone had realized that there was no other food. There were tough days that we felt like it's the end. Many bodies were shaded by anything and looking at us with lost looks. I didn't know what and how did happen? However, I knew very well that the situation had become worse than to be accepted or bearable.

I was continuing to read the overlapping sentences when my husband, Fahd, came in and delighted us with the sweets he had brought, and my mother-in-law began to pray and praise him. The children had eaten as much as they could, and my mother-in-law was looking at them and laughing. Not only that, but he promised us an outing to Rabwah's orchards upon his friends' advice. The children were happy and applauded for his sudden suggestion. After the little ones has slept, I went up to the room, I know it's Thursday, so I got ready for him. His ecstasy this time was double, perhaps because it was preceded by eating the delicious sweets. Then, he had slept deeply.

We woke up late. His face was full of happiness and contentment, and how couldn't he be like that; I felt him almost eat my body because of his yearning for it. My mother-in-law prepared breakfast with what my father-in-law has brought of beans, hummus, and falafel. I noticed that my father-in-law was peeping at my husband, as he had caught his attention, devouring quickly his food. I understood what these looks have meant, so I tried to alert him, as his actions almost foreshadowed what we have done yesterday. Laziness has dominated his body, and how couldn't he be after all this? Consequently, he changed his suggestion from an outing to Rabwah to a visit to the Umayyad Mosque, which is closest to us. Of course, my mother-in-law has supported him right away, and then everyone has successively supported and praised this suggestion.

We went into the Hameediya market from the middle after we crossed the Mid'hat Pasha market. The children were fascinated by what they saw of various exhibits and merchandise. We stopped at the licorice seller at the entrance to the Warrakeen market. My father-in-law had freshly drunk the entire cup, and my husband did as well, and then we continued our walk to the Umayyad Mosque. My mother-in-law had prayed several times, perhaps because of the place spirituality. As for me, I hastened to finish my prayer to control my children, as their movement made some noise in the place. My husband used to pray next to my father-in-law away from us, and then they joined us to continue our outing.

This was our first visit to the Umayyad Mosque, so my husband started explaining to my mother-in-law about the shrine of the Prophet "Yahya", while the children were playing in the mosque's courtyard near the well. We felt hungry, so my mother-in-law brought out what she has carried of fresh brioche that my husband had previously bought and distributed to us. We were laughing and were very happy. Then we visited the shrine of our master Imam Al-Hussein's head, so my mother-in-law said to my husband: "Do you see my son that injustice had always existed with humans; they didn't only cut off Yahya's head, but Al-Hussein also, even though he's the Prophet Mohammed's grandson."

My father-in-law added: I swear by God, I don't know how a Muslim could kill the Prophet's grandson?

My mother-in-law nodded her head and said: Abu Fahd, injustice has no religion. Injustice is the darkness, and the oppressor is so blind.

I was engrossed in their conversation. Sometimes I found in my mother-in-law, despite her simplicity, a high philosophy that I didn't read in books. Later, we went back home after we had bought the wooden clogs we need, some spices, and incense sticks.

I thanked God after I have known about Sheikh Ibrahim's family travel, as his brother-in-law had come and taken them all to his wife's father's house in Raqqa. We didn't hear anything else about them. People were tired and life and death had become equal for them. People had reported many stories of hunger, treachery, and death. Life had begun to form strange and different scenes from what we had known, while bodies were falling one by one. The women's wailing was no longer loud behind funerals, for death was always present wherever we go in the houses and the streets.

Hundreds of men, including me, have lined up on the river's sides. We have raced to win anything edible, even if it was a frog or a dead animal. Some have dived deeper into the river, hoping of catching the insidious fish, which they over-hidden from us. It seems that they realized their bleak fate when the river passed through the city. I saw the men quarreling carelessly over a fish smaller than the palm; it had become the usual and painful scene as well. I was robbed several times, on my way back to my home, I didn't want to defend myself, not even to know the faces disguised with a torn shemagh. I only left to them what was in my hand of hard and old loaves of bread, and returned safely to my home. I closed the door to my room. I was afraid to be killed during those attempts of robbery and looting, which have become common in recent times.

The soldiers had increased the high walls fortifications, and if hadn't it been for the fear of impalement, the people would have rushed towards them with their sticks and fists. The Turks were trained to read minds, so their actions weren't arbitrary in vain, for the impalement, with its cruelty, has constituted real terror in all people, so they succumbed to oppression, no matter how severe it was. The view was brutal, a body dripping blood in the death session on a stick that pierced him from his buttocks to his mouth or even his shoulders.

The cemetery wasn't far away, but it was adjacent to the city, so I had often seen the coffins waddling with the dead bodies inside it. I would have to postpone eating the hard loaf of bread that I had brought and hid it in my clothes folds on my way home, until after I had read a book so that I could get out of my constant nausea. The pace of that continued for some moment, sometimes to an unbearable point, and sometimes it passed with the patience that the Creator bestowed upon us. I longed for Uncle Ezra's wisdom, with its false optimism, or even for Hannah's boring and naive tales.

I came to Yuzbashi Jamal's office upon a prior appointment. He had a guest who spoke Arabic slowly and with a strange accent. Yuzbashi Jamal has asked me to perform a haircut for him, so I did it. His hair was soft and smooth, and then he suggested to him, to have cupping after the haircut, praising my ingenuity in front of him, so I remained in my place until he agreed to that. After he put on his clothes, I felt him move gracefully, and he said that he felt as if a great weight had been removed from his back. He was generous with me, for he gave me more than I deserved, despite Yuzbashi's opposition. I had previously seen a foreign guest with him, and I understood from what happened between them that they came to study the topography of the region and its historical monuments.

On my way back I was stopped by a person who swore to me that he hadn't eaten anything for several days. There was no more garbage, everything had been eaten, and even the cats' tolls had suddenly decreased. I don't know if they died? Or did someone cook them? There were no more dogs barking at night, as usual, perhaps they were busy digging up recent graves and enjoying the emaciated bodies buried in them. Everything in the city was frightening, and it didn't pass a day that we hadn't been surprised by a crueler and bitter day.

I was no longer caring about the sun rising as much as I did about its setting, for sleep had become a pleasure that bring us out of life's hardships. Only the books that I had kept, have made me feel like I'm a human being and I'm still alive. I have read some of the stories that have described Baghdad, its beauty, and its secrets, while others have spoken of people and their tendencies. The Euphrates River was flowing indifferently to the hungry city status. The days have passed amid frightful anxiety and have increased with what we call skirmishes between the policemen and the looters. Some bodies have been impaled after killing them to strike terror in their souls. Only the rain might wash away the sins, spread serenity, and restore life to its cycle that had almost stopped.

It caught my attention that something was happening far from the city, and what I found in the police camp was foreshadowed an important thing to happen. I tried to take my mind off what I saw so as not to get caught up in guessing that might be right or wrong. Gossip and speculation had abounded, so I went on my way despite what I heard from them.

The grumbling against the soldiers had reached a great extent, but it was the impalement, that strange tool that penetrates the body violently had killed and silenced hundreds or even thousands of mouths at the same time. Yes, the impalement alone, that invention that has proved its sustainable success, and without it, the masses might have attacked the soldiers, killed and crushed them. The city's notables had been preoccupied with donating to import grain to feed the hungry mouths, which had been obviously increased.

On my last visit to Yuzbashi Jamal, it caught my attention his concern, which I didn't notice before, "confirming what was said that something had happened and had shaken the Sublime State's pillars." He looked cranky and nervous; I couldn't even look into his eyes while I was with him. I felt that he wanted to relax more than having a haircut, as his body's veins were obviously twitching. I massaged his head several times until he calmed down a bit. He gestured to me with his hand to get out, so I quickly got out and breathed a sigh of relief for I walked away from him.

I was about to reach the house when I was stopped by a woman whom I didn't know, but who seemed to be a "prostitute" working secretly. I felt that she wanted to barter for some of what I had, so I invited her to my house to secretly agree on what we wanted. The street was empty of pedestrians when she came in and shut the door after me. We didn't argue for a long time, as she has quickly showed me the goods that my body had needed.

With a quick movement, she bared the lower part of her body and turned around to turn her back towards me, she was in a hurry, and as soon as I finished she lowered her dress on my thighs; she has given me a cheap good that matched the meager wage she received from me, and went out quickly, disregarding even to look at the place where she has got naked in. I also disregarded her because she wasn't the type that forces you to remember it.

I don't know what has happened to us to do these things silently and oppressively. I lay down on my bed alone, recalling some memories. I missed my father, that loyal friend who I missed his faint voice and his distinctive hoarseness.

I was very tired so I went to my room after the children have slept and I slept too. I heard his footsteps' sounds, but the fatigue has prevented me from getting up. I felt him lying down next to me, so I moved away a little to let him have a more space. Then, I turned my back to him and fell asleep. It wasn't his habit to come in so late at night; he lay down next to me and I felt his naked body after he lifted my dress and clung to me. I wished things would end here. He kissed my hair and tried to wake me up, and when he despaired, he stuck to me. I don't like these selfish acts that derive from coercion as a way to reach the goal.

I indeed had no legitimate excuse for refraining from fulfilling his desires, but I was tired and so exhausted. I have cooked for them, and washed a mountain of white and colored clothes, cleaned the house, and taught the children their lessons. After all this, am I not entitled to a peaceful sleep in the corner of my bed? His actions had bothered me, as he didn't stop, but rather he turned me on my back and fell on me with his heavy weight, and I didn't utter a word. He tried to have sex with me coercively; he couldn't at first, but after several attempts, he got of me.

I have felt him inside, but it wasn't the usual feeling, rather it was like a heavy load holding my breath with annoying tingles of his pubic hair. A few moments had passed until I was able to go back to sleep. I didn't reproach him in the morning, even though he forced me to take a bath with cold water because of what he has done with me. I know that I'm his wife and he has rights over me, but what he did was coercion and unjustified aggression against me.

I have avoided his looks at me. He was high and happy, telling jokes and sarcastic comments without justification. My mother-in-law has realized what was wrong with me; it seems that she had lived the same before. The poor woman has repeatedly tried joking with me; I have exchanged smiles with her and said to myself: It wasn't your fault; he had done it very simply, and he didn't bother himself to wipe his semen that flooded me or even to adjust my dress to cover my buttocks; perhaps if we had no common quilt, my thighs might have remained bare until I cover them myself.

I occupied myself with preparing the children to go to school, and I had a quick bath to wash everything that has stuck on me, and I went back to the scrolls, reading them again and repeating what my mother-in-law said: "Whoever sees the others' misfortune, his misfortune will be easier for him."

She said it while was talking to my father-in-law about the misfortune of her widowed relative who had recently lost her son. I couldn't continue to listen to their dialogue as I delved deeper into the events in these scrolls that were full of strange things.

People had been divided among themselves with frequent reports of the battles that had raged in the south of the Ottoman Sultanate. Many jokes, satirical and implicit comments had begun to circulate in the narrow lanes far from the police's ears. Everyone had been wanted to get out of this difficult situation, there were many taxes, and most of the men had been driven to war and life had been completely disrupted and poverty had driven people to the point of unbelief.

I had been confronted again by a woman who I didn't see her face because she had stipulated that. She followed me until we came into the house alone. I had been ashamed of myself for what I did, and I don't know why I did it. She had insisted on keeping her clothes and covering her face. I got closer to her and when I started to undress her, she started crying. I was on my knees, and then I sat in amazement. She muffled her voice with her palm, so I approached her again, I had been completely aroused, but as soon as I have bent on her, she started crying and wailing again. This time I stayed away from her, I couldn't do anything. Moments later, she asked me to hurry up and finish it because she had left her children starving. I turned away from her, and she was afraid that she might come back empty-handed. She has lifted her dress with her hands and said nervously: Hurry up, I must go home. Therefore, I realized what she was in; I stopped what I was going to do and gave her what I promised her. She quickly took it and left.

That night I have dreamed of Sarah that she had visited me and compensated me with more pleasure. It had been a sweet dream that I had got pleasure from as if it was true. I woke up looking for her, but I realized that it has been only a dream about a body.

The next day I went to the riverside to fish, but I failed, several hours I had spent waiting in vain. There was a compassionate fisherman who had sat next to me and had given me a medium-sized fish. I apologized for accepting it, but he insisted to. He was an old man, so I took the fish and said goodbye to him. I hastened with it to my house to clean it and grill it, but my joy wasn't complete, as Hannah's friend has visited me and shared it with me.

She began to complain about her difficult conditions, as there were no longer men in the city, and there was no money and no livelihood except with the police officers. She asked me to allow her to stay all overnight, so I agreed. She slept in the small room, but as soon as it got dark, she got infiltrated into my bed on the pretext that she has feared darkness. I let her stick to me and do whatever she has wanted. Consequently, I realized the horror of what happened after the men had been led to the war. Yeah, life had been completely disrupted, and things had turned upside down. However, how long will the situation remain like this and how long will people be able to withstand and endure. We didn't talk a lot between us except during the breaks after the rounds of having sex that has extended until the morning.

I was surprised by the house landlord's relatives' request that I should vacate the house because they need it, even though I had been committed to paying the rent on time. I have shortened the discussion with them hoping by giving me some time, as the current circumstances are difficult. I wished if she didn't die so that I wouldn't see such people, so as soon as they buried her they have rushed to divide the inheritance among themselves. I think that they have intended to sell it, as it wasn't reasonable for all of these people to share the simple rent. I went to her older brother and explained to him my situation, so he agreed that I might stay for a while, while I might manage my affairs, for he knew the extent of my commitment to pay the rent to him after her husband's death.

The rough nature of Deir Ezzor's people had made me bewildered, sometimes I thought that their reactions were hatred or malice, and then I have found out that they had their character that they had been characterized and that their frankness had interceded for them, for they speak without equivocation and their intentions are clear. I remembered that poor peasant who had hosted me when I came to Deir Ezzor. Poverty had brought us together, so we had got closer to each other, but as soon as he knew that I was a Jew, he has moved away and preferred self-distancing. We didn't argue about that and he tried to hide it although it seemed obvious and yet he provided me with enough food that day

I didn't hate poverty because of the humiliation of need, but because it created a rift and division in society as well. It wasn't like religion or nationalism; it was a special case that resulted in many effects. My grandfather's disagreement with the Damascenes wasn't that he was alien to them, as there were many merchants and those who were privileged who were also strangers to the city. It wasn't also because he had disagreed with the rabbi who had prevented him from visiting Mount Gerizim before he asked his permission, but rather because he was poor. This poverty had suddenly afflicted him after losing his trade. He thought that his move to Damascus might introduce him to another society, as there were no gloating glances at him that might follow him wherever he went. However, he had learned too late that fates may continue to follow us wherever we go. My grandfather had died of oppression created by miscreants, and my father, that poor peaceful man, had died because of the life that had shorn him with all its weight and burdens as well.

Joy has prevailed with the soldiers' departure from the city, and indeed from the entire country, only a few people have expressed their sympathy with them. Things have recovered a little, for they have left with their abhorrent taxes that don't end "the tax of a new ruler's arrival, the tax of celibacy, marriage, and births, as well as a tax on trees, on the land and the same tax on the property and the rooftop and even on the doors and..... and......etc... ".

The city's notables had been among the best of its men, whom the common people had been satisfied with them. They have carried on consultations among themselves to run the city's affairs, with no goal or interest to them except safety and security. As for those soldiers, they were strangers from all corners of the earth, and they were the coercive power tools to tighten their oppressive grip. People have breathed a sigh of relief; perhaps it was the hope of a future less bleak than what they went through. They were difficult days that will be passed down through generations as a harsh and unforgettable lesson. The city's notables have gathered to control matters in it, its men were armed to defend it to any robbery or looting actions; so arms had been distributed to those who had shown their willingness to defend it.

The relationship between the city's people and the surrounding clans had been strange. They were cousins. Nevertheless, *these clans that lived outside the city might invade and loot them from time to time. The city's notables had been the clans' sons, and because their decisions were collective, and done after extensive deliberation among them, so they were characterized by wisdom and foresight. They had known very well that the bandits are small groups, and as soon as they might know that there were who guards the city or defending it; they might hurry to withdraw, dragging their disappointment with them.*

When the countryside's men and the desert's people had visited me, I was aware of the hidden hostility in their hearts against the city's people, perhaps because of the sarcastic comments they had heard from them, or because they had felt unfair when they bartered with them. They were simple societies to the point of naivety. During work with Uncle Ezra, he informed me about many secrets of the city and the countryside. He was a seasoned merchant, and some of them preferred to deal with him to detest Deir Ezzor's people. This speech was ambiguous to me, as the same person might become a target to the other through his belonging. Thus, if they were from the same clan, this becomes "Deiri" and that "countryside man" becomes "Shawi", even though they were both of the same origins. Most of Deir Ezzor's residents were clans that have settled there, and some neighborhoods were even named after those who have inhabited them. Sometimes, I find that they had a love of rivalry, so they looked for conflict reasons between them, which support their opinion and fuel permanent conflicts between them.

My father-in-law has sipped the mint infusion I had prepared for him, and my mother-in-law kept picking mint leaves from the courtyard as I continued peeling and slicing the potatoes. My father-in-law has praised the infusion taste. My mother-in-law chewed on the small leaves that were in her hand and said: Who did eat the mint that I planted in the garden?

My father-in-law immediately replied: Who might be other than the Jews? Wish the poison shreds their bodies.

- Don't curse them.

- I swear by God, I'll curse them and I'll keep praying, God damn them, they had displaced and had expelled us from our homes and had forced us out, how couldn't I curse them; they had slept in our homes and had eaten from our trees.

- We also lived here in their homes, and the mint that we are eating is from their home courtyard, and they may be cursing us because we lived in their house.

- And who had started it, weren't they the ones who had expelled us and we came here, God may bless those who had helped us.

- But those were different than the other ones.

- They were all Jews, may God curse them.

- A hundred times, I told you don't curse the Jews, but the ones who had expelled us. Curse the ones who had expelled us from our country, not all Jews were the same, these were different from those. Like when we came out by force, they also came out by force.

-May God curse the one who caused it. It will keep burning in my heart to go back to my home and make my food from my garden.

- God is generous; the Arab forces have told us: Don't take anything with you, just two days and you'll go back to your homes.

- You have believed them and we went out.

- All people have believed them and came out.

- I wonder if they were accomplices, or were follies.

- God knows I can't doubt them.

- Is it possible that they have betrayed us while they came to defend us?

- I swear by God, I don't know where the truth is. Some have said that they were traitors, and others have said that they were fooled like us.

- Like us! Did anyone ask us our opinion?

- I meant they were fooled like us, and we came out.

- I wished we died and didn't come out.

- This is what I said, the soul is precious, and if we don't care about ourselves, otherwise we should care about children. I came out for my son won't die.

- Don't remind me of our sorrows, this was what had happened, let's forget.

- Forget alone. I won't forget until I die. How do I forget my homeland and my brothers who I didn't see again? I'll continue to curse against the Jews for the last day of my life.

- Curse as you want on the ones who had expelled us, I told you, not all the Jews are the same.

- I'll curse and curse until I return to my homeland, or until God took me away. Did you like the second one?!!

- Which second one, my dear?

- God took me away?

- This is not my concern.

- I didn't hear you whishing evil stay away from me. Maybe, you said Amen secretly.

- It's enough, I can't bear more sorrows.

- As you like, I'll prepare the lunch.

I used to witness their conversations that sometimes end with one of them angry and upset, and I also used to lower my head, preoccupied with what I'm doing so that I might not be struck by the arrows of unjustified interference between them. I prepared some fried food with some omelets, for everyone loves it.

This is the second time that I have re-read Al-Jahez's[25] Animal Book. It's a huge book, but it's interesting and contains various tales and an accurate description in a humorous way. I saw it as an encyclopedia with its varied and important information and in an interesting style to the extent that one never tires of reading it, as it talks about everything. It had illuminated some dark corners for me and I learned more about the mysteries of man, animals, and plants.

At first, the books were my only amusement, but later they have turned into a very important daily activity. Yes, they have distracted me from my work a bit, but they have given me all the information I had needed. That had been my father's advice to me to read...and then, read. It had been his habit to read in a low voice, and if he noticed my presence, he raised his voice to share with me what he was reading. So, if he felt that I was listening, he might explain to me what he reads so that I could understand it completely. He told me that the vision isn't complete without reading, so the grace of sight with reading leads without the slightest doubt to better insight; he had always been right.

---

[25] Translator: a one of the prominent Arabic writer and scientific of Abbasid era.

Hajj Fadel's Government

I didn't realize at first what I have heard. Everyone was talking about forming a government whose headquarters and scope of work is this small city "Deir Ezzor". How? I don't know. The important thing was that it's a government.

Few people were happy with the news that had swept the city, for the first time this city might issue its decrees. There was no more Sublime Porte, neither Sultan nor the Grand Vizier. The government here had been headed by Hajj Fadel, the former mayor, who had left his post by a self-decision and formed a government with some notables to manage life's affairs. This government had become the most important talking among the Deir's people. The news had spread to the desert and to the countryside surrounding the city, so the Sheikhs of the clans had flocked to pledge allegiance and blessing.

Of course, I wasn't interested in what was going on unless it meant that I could return to my home in Damascus. Many jokes had added comfort and acceptance to the general atmosphere. Some had advised me to take the Prime Minister, Hajj Fadel's approval, but I hesitated to go to his council, even though I know him well. The army had terrorized us, even from ourselves and our acquaintances. One of my customers has volunteered to escort me. I had needed someone to escort me and calm me down when I would meet him face to face. We came into his office, and he greeted us delightfully. He was solemn and majestic as I had known him.

I let my companion explain my problem based on that they have the same character and kinship between them, and my intuition was correct. Hajj Fadel had agreed and expressed his readiness to help me.

I couldn't control myself in front of him, and I almost cried from my joy and kissed his hand in gratitude, we thanked him together and we left. I was like I had been released, and in fact, I was it. Indeed, Yuzbashi Jamal had frankly told me at that time, "you are under house arrest," this was how he pronounced it. Ah, how much freedom is wonderful...

At last, I'll return to my home, so I don't want to repeat my grandfather's mistake and spend my whole life crushed by the difficult alienation. I started preparing to travel to Damascus, waiting for the right opportunity to proceed. I have waited for a long time, maybe several weeks have passed during which I couldn't risk traveling, as I had to make sure that the road is completely safe due to the increasing of looting and robbery actions lately.

I was pleased with Ezekiel's arrival, for he was also late to come, fearing to be killed or stolen by the bandits. I have hosted him in my house and he was pleased with my desire to return to Damascus. He also couldn't bear to live more in Deir Ezzor, as he yearned to Aleppo, the city of pleasure, as he liked to call it. He had brought with him half the quantity of the goods that he used to trade in for fear of what might happen to him on the way. He sold all of them in Deir Ezzor and bought with their price wool and ghee to Aleppo. He has suggested that I go with him, and from there I might continue on my way to Damascus; I found it a suitable opportunity to see Aleppo, so I accepted his invitation and thanked him.

Aleppo

After I have arranged and finished all my affairs in Deir Ezzor, we set out with a convoy whose members were well known to Ezekiel and he was used to deal with them in the past. The road was tiring and long, but my feeling that I'm free eased the hardship of travel. Nonetheless, Ezekiel, with his sense of humor, gave us a comfortable atmosphere that we had needed, and despite the age difference between us, I felt like we are from one generation.

We have reached Aleppo after a long hard trip, and we went first to Hannah, who greeted us with a very warm welcome. I was pleased to see Maria in a good shape; it seemed that my prayers were answered along the way. I was very tired, so I went to the room that Hannah had prepared for us and fell asleep deeply. In the morning, I was surprised when Ezekiel came out of Maria's room, and it was clear that he had slept with her. I held back my anger at what had happened and convinced myself that there was no relationship between us and I have no right to show my jealousy about her. Ezekiel has continued his joking again as if nothing has happened.

We went together to the nearby markets to visit his friends, and he explained to me on the way his philosophy in life, so simply: "Live for your day and let tomorrow for tomorrow." As he said when he left his house in Baghdad, that he had completely forgotten those who he had left them there.

For this reason, as soon as he arrived in Deir Ezzor, he searched for who might make him forget who he had left in Iraq. So, as soon as he reached Aleppo, he did the same with Maria. Maria has become a prostitute, she's the hen who Hannah waits for her eggs every day.

He started explaining to me about Aleppo, which I was completely ignorant of. It has looked beautiful to me with its many and varied streets and markets. On our return, Hannah had prepared Aleppo's kibbeh for us, but Maria didn't share the food with us, and she remained in her room without explaining the reasons. In the evening she joined us for a sumptuous dinner with appetizers and araq. Ezekiel ate a lot and get drink too much, and then he took Maria by her hand, like an obedient wife to their ethereal nest. Then Hannah looked weirdly at me as if she would like to say something I didn't understand at all. My feet led me to her, I kissed her hands that fed me that delicious kibbeh, and she hurriedly embraced me like a small child.

I woke up at midnight on her snoring in different rhythms. I withdrew very quietly and began to find out and check the whole place. I was assured about Ezekiel's condition, as he was completely naked next to Maria, who had only covered a small part of her body; they had sex over and over again. I went back to Hannah and raped her by force because she was the one who had planned it. Although she was sleeping, she quickly accepted me and expressed her happiness at my physical violence, for I was oppressed and angry at the ways I had to take it by force. It was the first time that I avenge for myself, as the victim is destined to avenge a victim like her. At noon, Ezekiel asked if his house is ready for habitation, and Hannah told him that she had well cleaned and arranged it.

We moved to Ezekiel's house, which is adjacent to Hannah's house, but its main gate leads to another alley. Ezekiel has asked me if I would like to work with him, but I didn't answer him. He has noticed my hesitation and my disregarding. The next day we went to some of his friends. He skillfully did his commercial deals in a way that I hadn't known before. In the evening he gave me a good sum as well as a spacious separate room in his house for my fees.

Maria came in the evening, but I didn't notice her at first until she sat on my bed as I was lying down recalling my memories. I tried to hide my surprise at her arrival, as I didn't expect it at all. She didn't speak to me, but kissed me on the cheek several times and then pressed her lips to mine. I suddenly realized that I'm in Ezekiel's house and that she had become his concubine, so I moved away from her for a little; but she came back to me and kissed me more and more, and when she slipped under the quilt, I understood that she wasn't interested in Ezekiel or perhaps she was asked to doing that. I tried to get away from her even more because I had begun to comply with Ezekiel's will and dislike his wrath. She has noticed what I was in and understood it, so she whispered in my ear: Don't be afraid, Ezekiel had agreed with this. I don't know if it was the drowsiness that swept through my body or the sudden situation that made me in that state that I experience!

She didn't stop kissing and touching me until she reached the moment when she made my whole body spurt at once to top her with all its passion and lust. She had known that she would take me at that moment, so she slowly and persistently infiltrated with her feelings and movements inside me. Maria was more beautiful and sexier than I expected. She did wonders on that night, which its brilliance has extended until late hours. She withdrew the same as she came in complete silence. Then I fell asleep until the sun woke me up.

Although we had breakfast together, and then went to wander in the markets, but Ezekiel didn't seem that he knew what had happened. I don't know if he behaved with false disregarding, or he had something more important. Such was his nature. I used to accompany him like a shadow and I was enjoying it. Every moment I was with him made me more attached to him. He has a personality that combines a lot of contradictions, but he brings out only what he wants from them. He's a rare person I had never seen like him in my life. Sometimes, I find him very generous, not caring to spend everything he has, and sometimes he argues and bargains to win a grain of wheat.

We stopped on our way to Ezra's shop, it was the second time we visit it. He was tired and gentle. He offered me to work with him on the pretext of his weak health, so Ezekiel immediately laughed when he heard this, and then explained to Ezra when he noticed his strange looks because of his spontaneous laughter. He invited us to lunch, and we accepted his invitation and we came the next day.

That was the second time I see his daughter while she was embracing her little son by one hand and was grabbing her dress by another hand; she seemed to be different from that beautiful girl I had peeped at before. We had long conversations about Deir Ezzor and its secrets, some of which I was hearing for the first time. We missed Hannah in that sitting to tell us her most unusual stories.

In the evening, we went back to the house, and each of us went to his room. I was hoping that Maria would come to me to complete my ecstasy and happiness, but she didn't come.

During the morning breakfast, Ezekiel told me some funny situations that had happened to him; he intended to show me his savvy and experience in commerce. His extended itinerary from Baghdad to Aleppo and sometimes to Istanbul meant for him a forced trip that he had to invert it with his ingenuity and cleverness, to a wonderful outing, so he loves the Iraqi dishes "Bajah[26]", "Qeemah[27]", and Temmen[28]". However, at the same time, he yearns for "Deir Ezzor's okra stew", "Aleppo's kibbeh", and "Istanbul's kebab[29]"; this is how he had summarized them.

He made solid friendships that extended along his journey, so he knows where to eat "Mash'hamiyeh, Mamouniyeh[30], or Bajariyeh[31]." The obligatory breaks during his travels mean more

---

[26] Translator: sheep intestine and stomach stuffed with rice and minced meat.

[27] Translator: stew of chickpeas and meat.

[28] Translator: cooked rice with ghee.

[29] Translator: grilled meat.

[30] Translator: dessert made of semolina, butter, sugar, and topped with nuts.

[31] Translator: tandoori bread filled with pieces of grilled lamb, and served with green vegetables.

amusing and interesting conversations, in addition to the delicacies he used to taste.

In the evening, I heard voices coming from Ezekiel's room, I didn't intend to eavesdrop on them, but the voices were very clear. I was excited by those whispers in which it was clear that the other side was someone I don't know, neither Maria nor Hannah. Definitely, it was another girl. I wished that Maria had returned to visit me in my room, but she didn't. So, I closed my eyes, trying to recall the intimate meeting that had previously brought us together.

Ezekiel loves the boss role, which he masters perfectly, and he was more than happy that I accepted him. I had accepted all his lapses because he often follows them up with an apology or an endearing humorous demeanor. He had introduced me to the Jewish community that accepted my Judaism and rejected my Damascene until I told them the truth about my ancestors' coming from Egypt, and before that from Spain, so I found that warmth between them more than in Damascus, where the mysterious looks and the cold emotions.

I cut Ezekiel's hair, and I was glad he complied with my orders until I finished my work. He bowed his head in front of me for the first time and was unusually silent. The next day, after he complained to me about his back pain, I made for him the traditional recipe of cupping, and I left the phlebotomy procedure for another day. He was listening to me talking to him about its benefits and how to get cold air out of the body. He didn't argue with me about that, he remained submissive half-naked on his knees as I moved the bottles stuck to his back after anointing him with olive oil.

He let out a groan indicating that he liked my work and followed it with a larger one. He was giggling as if he was a small child when I was touching his sides and seemed happy as I knew him so that he said:

-I won't forget your favor, which is exactly what I had needed.

I told him of my intention to go to Damascus, but he begged me to stay for some time in his hospitality.

In the evening he sent me his special gift, it was a beautiful young girl. It seemed to me that she's new to her profession. We had a great time and we did that several times, during which I felt gazes on my back from the outside, but I disregarded them time after time until I caught Ezekiel was peeping on us.

He didn't justify this to me but he completely disregarded it, despite the convergence of our glances several times, as he continued watching our tender bodies' fusion. I didn't want to spoil the peaceful relationship between us over a slip he did it, even if it had bothered me, as its impact on me was less than the consequences of admonishing him.

Later on, we discussed the subject ambiguously. He told me that due to his old age, he can't have much sex, so he resorts to peeping on others to satisfy his desires and whims. As I'm always using to do, I supported him as a courtesy to him, but he considered this a desirable approval of this matter and took it to its end. Later it became clear to me that Maria and Hannah were fully aware of his peeping on them and had accepted it just as I did.

He had spread his gifts to everyone, so there was nothing wrong with what he did. So what was the harm in seeing their complete nudity, with or without a reason, wherever and whatever was, individually or collectively? Wasn't he the one who sponsored them and sheltered them with his experience? Hannah used with her experience to select for him, the most beautiful and obedient women, to present them to whomever he wanted from the merchants and those with good fortune. Thus, he was expanding his business and trade and increasing his profits to spread to everyone. Then, what was wrong if he inspected his followers and making sure of their bodies' shape and their good performance!?

Ezekiel has surprised me by his request to go with me to Damascus, I didn't expect that, but I was pleased with his decision, so going together would lessen on me the road hardship; we traveled as we agreed. When we arrived, I went straight to Abu Yusuf (Yusuf's father), who was my father's acquaintance. He welcomed my come back and helped me to open the door and clean the house.

Ezekiel was busy reading his book, so, Abu Yusuf found this an opportunity to get away from him. He blamed me for allowing people who have problems with the Sublime Ottoman State to rent my house. I explained to him the reasons for that, but he insisted on blaming me and reprimanding me and informed me that the police officers had taken them all, and if it wasn't for his testimony about me, I could have also been condemned with them to the death's journey to Istanbul. I didn't tell Ezekiel about what I heard; that was the first bad news I received about Sheikh Ibrahim's fate.

After that, the news has spread, and the most painful was the news of Sarah's marriage and her travel with her husband to Istanbul. Her mother joined them after that, and that was shortly before we arrived in Damascus. Ezekiel and I have wandered the markets of Damascus. I saw him criticizing it a lot and praising Aleppo and its markets. I didn't understand the reason for this comparison, which suddenly has abounded.

After we spent our second week in Damascus, he informed me of his desire to return to Aleppo, proposing to me and insisting on me sharing with him in his work, and explaining to me the profits and gains that I might reap if I agreed to that. Upon my request, we spent one more week in which Ezekiel was more critical of everything in Damascus until I completely hated it. I agreed with him on some of what he said, but his exaggerations seemed clear as the clarity of his intention behind it; I had no other choice, as the city had become strange to me after my father's death and Sarah's departure.

I agreed to return with Ezekiel to Aleppo. He smiled the victory's smile, as he was the one who used to be proud of his opinion's victory. He tried to relieve my sadness of Sarah's marriage, for he hates marriage with everything in it, for marriage for him is a permanent annoying prison. I said to myself: If you had ever seen her, your opinion might have changed completely.

When we left my house, I stood for a few minutes contemplating its gate and the small courtyard in front of it; the memories crowded in my head at once. Here we played and laughed and from here my father and I went out and came back together. From this gate, they took his corpse to his grave, and from that my beloved Sarah came out to a place I don't know.

For me, Damascus is where I see my father and I'm happy to talk to him, and where Sarah, my love, is my only love. I didn't look back. There was no longer any reason to invite me to that, as the house has become cold deaf walls, in which there is no warmth and lifelessness. I thanked God that Ezekiel was by my side when I heard the disturbing news and felt pain because of it.

We arrived in Aleppo shortly after the afternoon. Bahsita was preparing for the usual Saturday; and we also found rest after hardship. On Sunday morning, Ezekiel left the house without telling me about his destination, but apparently, he didn't want to leave me alone, so he instructed Maria to come to alleviate my sadness and depression; because she was used to her work, she quickly took off her clothes and lay down next to me. She was surprised that I stared at her for a long time. I looked for those features that I had seen one day, and I thought they were Sarah.

I wished she had stayed dressed, so I covered her up and stared at her again. Prostitution has covered her face with different powders until she became a girl other than the one I would like to kiss on that day. I couldn't find that innocence from her, so I slept with her, with my eyes closed, hoping to imagine her as Sarah. I got closer and attached to her, and she quickly accepted without any objection, so that it almost spoiled my pleasure, so she did it again with some rudeness. I was trying to delude myself that she's Sarah as if I was punishing her for her marriage and her travel to Istanbul.

I contemplated Maria's body after I got away from her; Sarah has what Maria has. I didn't forget her details and I still remember the most accurate ones. In fact, Sarah is much more beautiful and much fun. I wished she's beside me now, to kiss her splendid lips for a long time; I wished she's here with her complete nakedness and we attached as one body.

Maria, with her feminine sense and long experience, realized what I was in, so she started kissing my chest and my navel and went deeper into me. She was very skilled in sex to the extent that she was able to completely expel Sarah's spectrum from my imagination, so we were able to reach the ecstasy height.

We had a great time and took advantage of Ezekiel's absence to do sex again away from his peeping, but our joy wasn't completed, as he arrived and his successive cough alerted us to his presence. We tried not to stop and not to cover our bodies. This was a sin that we might be punished for later if we did it. When we realized that he moved away from us, we separated from each other to end this ridiculous play. Then, we all have gathered in the living room. He seemed indifferent to what he saw, as he started another conversation, and then Maria asked him permission to go and left.

Ezekiel surprised me by asking if I found Maria different this time. I didn't understand his question, so he explained to me that he meant if my feeling was glowing as it was in the first time I had sex with her. I replied to him negatively. Then, he added that this is his advice to me, as long as a person can renew his pleasure, why not do so.

I felt that he wanted to drag me to his philosophy, which I didn't understand, although I had to accept it because I had no other alternative. Ezekiel used to say: "We have to renew every day in our lives and no matter what, and we have always to look for something new and do it because repeating the same things periodically is a slow death." So he made it clear to me that my peeping on him wouldn't bother him at all, and he seemed to anticipate what would happen next.

The next day he brought a young girl, and it was the first time I see him naked from behind the glass. I felt that I was punishing him because he had done it a lot with me before. The girl was shy, but he had sex with her relentlessly; he wanted me to see the secrets of this thing, but I didn't realize his true intention. The next day, after we got back from work together, he started asking me many questions regarding what I had seen the night before. I was embarrassed and didn't know what to answer, so I asked him to clarify his questions. I know that I might not be able to repeat my peeping on him, because I didn't like that much, so I apologized to him, and told him that I did it in compliance with his previous orders. He was pleased with what I said and wanted me to elaborate more. I didn't have his talent for describing, so I laughed and told him that it was the normal view of bodies coming together to have sex. He ended his speech by praising the food and added: "One day you'll learn the secrets of the matter more".

We went together to Hannah's house, and we found her worrying about Maria, who was overwhelmed by depression and had isolated herself in her room. Ezekiel went to her room, but after half an hour he came back in vain, begging me to go to her, so I went. I said to myself: Ezekiel can't understand what is going with her because he had never been through it. She was alone squatted with lowered head. She didn't care about my coming and didn't reply to my greetings. I didn't know what to do?

It was a difficult task. All the tasks that Ezekiel had assigned to me were difficult, perhaps because they weren't in harmony with my nature. I yearn to live as I want, away from this strange atmosphere. I got closer to her, but she moved away to the corner where she lay down, looking tired and broken. I tried to kid with her, but she didn't respond. I tickled her waist, but she moved away. I tickled her waist again and strongly; she slapped me with all her strength, so I slapped her also and she shook and slapped me again while she was crying. I didn't know what happened to her, she was behaving crazily, so I slapped her so hard that my fingers have imprinted on her face. Thus, she cried more and when I tried to get closer to her, she cursed me with dirtier words and qualities.

I came out of the room to be surprised by Ezekiel. He was peeping at us, but he seemed silent and sad. He asked Hannah not to leave Maria alone, and we went out together. We passed by a man playing with a monkey and with him a boy of ten years old. We stood watching his movements; Ezekiel tried to control himself from laughing and then exploded with audible giggles, as did I and most of the crowd that surrounded them.

After we ate some grilled kibbeh that we had bought from a small shop, he asked me why I slapped her. I told him that I couldn't control myself, so he answered me that our work required self-control, and she has already borne our foolishness and impudence. He paid attention to my lack of understanding of his phrase, so he clarified that it's not easy for a woman to sell her body for whatever reasons. We may see her doing it easily, but in her innermost, she suffers from it.

It seemed that he wanted to elaborate more on the subject, but a friend of his suddenly interrupted his speech and greeted him. They spoke in front of me, and later then he moved aside, and they talked about something that Ezekiel didn't tell, and I didn't ask him. On our way back, Ezekiel bought the sweets that Maria loves, and we went home together. He asked me to present it to her and to pretend that I was the one who brought them, and to reconcile her; so I did it.

She has cried again and slapped me and got mad again, but I controlled myself more. She slapped me while I was putting the kunafa[32] in her mouth. I tried not to care about her unjustified slaps until she smiled. She took three large pieces in her hand and put them all at once in my mouth. I almost choked when she forcefully pressed them. I said to myself: If she only slapped me, it was easier than what she did. Then she giggled loudly until Hannah and Ezekiel came to find out what was going on. I hoped to get out of this madness, but I complied with Ezekiel's orders and controlled myself. Consequently,

---

[32] Translator: very famous dessert made with white melded cheese topped with baked semolina or vermicelli.

we all came into the living room, and we continued talking and laughing and eating sweets as if nothing had happened.

My father-in-law suddenly burst into tears while was listening to the patriotic anthem (Oh My Homeland), and soon my mother-in-law's tears also have fallen. It was a difficult scene as if we are leaving our homes now. We didn't look at each other's faces, but each turned back to himself, listening and repeating in his heart what he heard. When I deeply listened to the lyrics of the memorable anthem, I realized that there was a special rhythm that it transmits in the soul to do all this melodious feeling. I re-read the lyrics more than once, they are simple words, and directly interfere with the heartbeat:

Shall I see you safe blessed; victorious and honored,

Shall I see you; eminent, reaching the stars,

Oh my homeland, oh my homeland…

In that family session, I felt from my father-in-law's looks and tears that we had lost something so precious and difficult, and then we went to sleep. I recapitulated some of what I read; many phrases forced me to go back to what I had previously read. I asked my husband again about that thing he put in the bag and he took it out in a hurry and again evaded answering me clearly and frankly. I would like to tell him that one day I might find a true answer to my questions and I might re-read every letter Kislev had written, and I might find a reason one day to go down to that basement and decipher its riddles and talismans.

The children have quickly adapted to the new life in this neighborhood, to the extent that the Levantine dialect infiltrated a lot in their conversations. This interference in their daily conversations made me laugh with the overlap of their accustomed dialect with the dialect that surrounded them in the school and the neighborhood. Even my husband started using some expressions as a joke sometimes or unconsciously at other times. Only my mother-in-law insisted on attaching to her dialect, correcting for the children from time to time, thinking that they pronounce incorrectly, amid the giggles of my father-in-law, who agreed with her at times and disagreed with her at other times.

She saw this as the beginning of accepting the idea of our permanent presence here and our forgetting of Palestine over time. My father-in-law was very indifferent to her exaggerated fantasies as well as my husband, who began to integrate more into this society, starting with bringing the hookah to smoke on the rooftop, passing through many of the daily habits that he began to implement. My father-in-law brought a lot of small plants and planted them in the courtyard's pots, and put some of them in pots on the stairs, and little by little the number of plants began to multiply until we felt as if we were in a beautiful garden.

Ezekiel has traveled to Baghdad, and I was needed to ask Ezra about everything before I act; Ezekiel had left his shop after emptying the goods which he had taken with him to Baghdad. I was able to meet with Maria far from Hannah and Ezekiel's snooping. We spent a lot of time, and she complained to me about her suffering with Hannah in her broken Arabic accent, but she begged me not to tell Hannah about her talking and secrets. She knows that Hannah was using her body most horrifically. She told me about those who had forcibly slept with her with their filthy bodies and their filthiest words, to the extent that she now hates this matter. She told me dozens of stories that were almost unbelievable about what these people did to her, and Hannah received the price while she was bearing their dirtiness and savages.

She told me that she was raped many times because some men don't enjoy sex unless with rape and that she had suffered greatly from their rudeness, harshness, and profanity. As for Hannah, her actions were limited to treating her wounds and patting her shoulder to accept it again. What she hated the most was Ezekiel's snooping on her, as this has afflicted her innermost and caused pain and annoyance, which she only accepted under compulsion. At first, she tried to object, but Ezekiel's expensive gifts made her completely acquiesce to him, and she was afraid to leave them because there was nowhere else to go.

Ezekiel had completely controlled her, sometimes was kind and another time was cruel.

She told me that what bothers her most about Ezekiel is his strange behavior, which she has never been accustomed to. His enjoyment of peeping on her when having sex with others who were completely ignorant of that and her knowledge of it made her extremely annoyed and angry at the same time. In her view, Ezekiel is the smartest and most intelligent human being who makes you willing to do whatever he wanted without any objection.

It was more than a week since Ezekiel's travel. I bought for him the goods that he would take with him to Baghdad next time, using Ezra's instructions and Hannah's strict supervision of me, who then informed me of a regular visit to Ezekiel's friend. So, I have to stay at her house during the days he would stay in Ezekiel's house. I complied with her words, and took my things, and dwelt in a room in her house. Hannah cleaned the house and prepared it for him; Maria stayed with him to be at his service. That's what Hanna has said, even if she meant a lot by saying that.

I didn't see him and didn't recognize him. I know that she might tell Ezekiel the details of our actions in his absence, so I disregarded what happened as if it didn't concern me. The biggest burden was on the poor Maria. I moved to a similar room but another house. As for her, she moved to a room with a stranger, and she has to obey him and accept him as he is. Throughout his stay, Hannah has prepared fine food. I should have tasted it first and then she carried it to the dear guest.

I tried to isolate myself in the room and read some of what I found in Ezekiel's library. Hannah allowed me this isolation at times and embraced me at other times to listen to her many stories or to massage her legs with her prominent varicose. The guest's stay didn't last long, after which Maria returned with an expensive golden bracelet in her hand, which seemed to be a reward for her good performance with him. I went back to sleep in Ezekiel's house, according to his prior orders.

After more than a week, I visited Hannah who was very confused and was concealing something. I didn't ask her despite my concern about what she had until she said what she had hidden. Maria had run away. She said it, angrily and convulsively. I had to stay to console her, for she was experiencing sad and depressing moments. I hugged her with my body to change her mood into a happy and pleasant atmosphere.

I went back to Ezra to help him with many things, and he was very generous with me. He knows that I hate working behind the wooden loom and I only did it for him. One day when I was cutting his hair in his shop, he told me that his shop was large and that he might divide it among us, so I might be close to him and thus help him from time to time. I told him that there were tasks entrusted to me and that I had to accomplish in fulfillment of Ezekiel's orders, so he added: I don't think he would mind, however, I'll wait for him to come back.

Maria's news had reached Hannah. She was a little comforted when she told me, that Maria was caught with someone when they were having sex, and it seems that it wasn't the first time. So, Maria was sent to the brothel and Hannah was waiting for Ezekiel's come back to do the necessary about this matter. It seemed that the things waiting for Ezekiel began to increase with time and we all have nothing to do but to wait.

I woke up to loud and repeated sounds hitting the mortar, so I went out to investigate that sound. Hannah was venting her anger by placing wheat grains in the mortar and smashing them with a wooden pestle. It was clear that she was in pain and sadness. She prepared for us a strange dish consisting of cooked wheat and bacon. I had never tasted anything like it; perhaps she made up this kind of food to get out of the case that recently afflicted her. I tried to pretend that it was delicious to satisfy her. However, she followed me with her malicious looks while I was eating, and she repeatedly asked about its taste.

There is no doubt that Maria is happy now. I said to myself. Hannah came closer and stared at me more as if she wanted to read *what was inside me. She was silent and then said: Poor Maria, you couldn't longer keep your thighs closed later then.*

I couldn't control myself, so some granules came out of my mouth to my sudden laughter, so I quickly picked them up with my hand. The brothel wasn't far from us, but it's also in Bahsita. She asked me to go to Maria, but I suggested to her that's better to wait for Ezekiel's return, and she reluctantly agreed to my suggestion.

I visited Ezra many times and congratulated him for his new grandson's birth. He was so happy about this event and he insisted on me eating several pieces of sweets he brought to celebrate the occasion. I said to myself, how much I wished I was that child's father, and I wished Ezra's daughter was my wife, that all my problems and obsessions would have ended.

Good job in the shop that he prepared for me, and a beautiful wife who expels my tiredness with wonderful food and a delicious body. How wonderful to play with your child in the morning and your beautiful wife in the evening. But, what if I died or my wife died? Then the same tragedy would be repeated and a child like me will go into eternal misery.

Ezra pulled me out again from what I was in, while he was insisting on a new piece of sweet, which I took and thanked him. Ezra returned to work weaving a new rug from the old clothes he had brought. He gave me some copper pieces that Ezekiel had recommended to include in the rest of the things we collect for him.

Hannah asked me again to visit Maria to check on her, so I told her that the presence of the gendarmerie might cause us problems that we couldn't handle and bear, and it's better to wait for Ezekiel's return to decide the best. Ezekiel's name was enough to support any proposal that I put forward.

Hannah tried to occupy herself by preparing the food she could master. She's a skilled cooker, I liked all that she has served except for those dishes that didn't have a specific name, and I think she mixed the ingredients hoping that she might make a new delicious recipe attributed to her one day, and I was her experiments' field. For example, she once tried to make Mamouniyeh from bulgur or rice, and she failed, as she had done in all the previous innovations. The strangest thing was that she completely forgot the ingredients she had previously used to use for the same recipe.

Her madness was coming out of her and settling in the little pieces I had to eat. Some of them were palatable, while the hunger was compelling me to eat the others. Finally, Ezekiel arrived carrying dates, delicious molasses, and most importantly some books and manuscripts. He was surprised by the disturbing news, as his advice to us was always to avoid any action that may cause problems.

Ezekiel followed Maria's subject in the following days and told us that he would work to get her out of the brothel and return her to the house. We have visited Ezra, who also briefed him on some matters. We talked for a long time about the upcoming news of the Promised Homeland Project.

In the evening, he told me that it was difficult to get Maria out of the brothel unless she got married. He said that he was thinking of a solution to the matter, but the dilemma he would encounter was that she would still be under surveillance for a long time and might cause us more trouble in the future, so we have to wait and study the matter thoroughly. He was interested in her, but he was also afraid of the consequences, so he was so careful about dealing with this matter. We spent the following days buying and selling, and I used to see him bringing a new girl permanently, as well as peeping on us as usual after that.

The news came of Maria's murder at the hands of a client who tried to rob her after having sex with her. The poor woman was stabbed several times and the offender cut off her hand after it was impossible for him to remove the golden bracelet from her hand. Hannah was severely depressed, and so did Ezekiel and I, and the whole house were sad. Later, we followed up on our business because Ezekiel's trip became very near. We were able to buy most of his *orders. Hannah was so happy and finally, she laughed after hearing Ezekiel's approval to accompany him on his next trip to Baghdad.*

I spent some days alone until one of Ezekiel's mistresses visited me, and I knew that he had asked her to do so. Her presence reminded me of him, as I had become addicted to the pleasures that I learned from him, so I worked day and night to be able to spend on women. Sometimes, after I finish having sex and the girl leaves the house, I curse Ezekiel in my heart and the day I knew him since he made me repeatedly committing this. I became a slave to my instincts and this ugly weekly act became a part of my life. I no longer trust women, they are all whores in my opinion, so I distanced myself from the marriage's idea and having children, for I didn't want to repeat my tragedy, and I followed what I read to Al-Ma'arri[33]:

"This was what my father sinned against me, and I didn't sin against anyone."

I won't be the cause of my children' misery. I'll adopt Ezekiel's philosophy or some of it and go on with life on his approach. Ezekiel's visits made me happy, for he used to make me laugh with his lewd jokes and actions. This time he brought a girl with him to serve us. I was saddened by the news of Hannah's illness, which made her completely paralyzed. With Ezra's assistance, Ezekiel was able to sell the house, which I found out, was the real landlord, not Hannah. He told me that the incoming international news has predicted the occurrence of future surprises, and that we should prepare for them. Ezra has agreed to that when he repeated his speech in front of him, but he told him that he refuses to leave Aleppo, for it's the city where he was born, lived, and he wants to die and be buried in. I took advantage of Ezekiel's presence in Aleppo and offered him to accompany me to go to Damascus, but he apologized. He told me that he started to believe the rumors and he had considered selling all his properties.

---

[33] Translator: an Arabic poet and philosopher of Abbasid era.

I returned alone to Damascus and spent several days there. Finally, I knew some of what had happened to me, as some of my acquaintances confided to me that Sarah's mother, through her many acquaintances, especially those with influence and authority, was the one who had asked the vice governor to forcibly deport me to Deir Ezzor. They were angered by her action, but they couldn't do anything other than cut off their relationship with her, which forced her to travel to her daughter Sarah in Istanbul.

Some of them tried to apologize to me for what had happened, but their cold feelings towards me made me the same as them, so I didn't respond to what I heard. Therefore, I went back to Aleppo. Ezekiel had sold his house and was preparing to go back to Baghdad. Ezra was somewhat pleased with that, which meant that I'll work with him, and I did, but I told him that my stay in Aleppo is temporary and might be for a short period because I think to go back permanently to Damascus. I was confused, and if hadn't been for him, I would have gone back immediately.

The political turmoil engulfed Syria, and it reminded us of what Ezekiel had told us, but Ezra was repeating his words by clinging to Aleppo no matter what happened, and he remained committed to his words until that fateful day when he fell from his wooden chair while was doing his usual work. We tried to help him, but fate was quicker than us.

I felt with his pass away that an important part of me had left with him. I spent several days after his burial recalling our memories together. I'll never forget those days that had begun with my acquaintance with him. I was lost and drowning in my sorrows and homeless in a rural city of which I was completely ignorant, and I had never heard of it before, nor had it even occurred to me that I would be forced to live in it. Ezra wasn't a simple person despite his feigning, but he was very intelligent, so he tried not to involve too much in the secret dealings with the police officers. He refused the slander and falsehood that some had done to get closer to them. This humanity that I touched with him brought me closer to him and I felt that he too, from the moment he shook my hand, found something with me that made him bring me closer to him.

Our relationship went through many stages, not all of them were the same, on the contrary, they were contradictory and I didn't understand them sometimes. He showed some cruelty towards me to the point that I cried sometimes because of an unexpected reaction from him, and in return, he often pleased me with his supportive situations as much as he could. I was angry with some of his actions, some of them were justified, and others were first and foremost a human being's actions. The only crack that came between us was my marriage to his daughter, he wished to make her happy, and he wished for this marriage to continue in any case and had prepared himself to help us in various ways. I didn't blame him, any father would have done that for his daughter, and in turn, I hadn't angered him. He knows very well that I wanted to continue this marriage despite knowing that she wasn't the lover that I have wished.

I think that each of us sinned against the other, so we had forgiven what we had done to each other. Yes, our friendship was no longer the same as it was before my separation from his daughter, but there was also no hostility or hatred between us, we have lived our pain and tried to forget it. Oh, Uncle Ezra. How much I'm longing for a cup of tea with you in the afternoon, with its charming color, and your stories that send a delicious numbness in my body until I fall asleep.

I was working everyday hardly and tirelessly to enjoy those wonderful moments later. His wife didn't have the same tolerance as him, as I used to feel her hatred for me after what had happened, although it has decreased over time. I continued working in Ezra's shop, according to his family's wishes. The general situation was unstable and tainted by many ambiguities.

One day, I passed by the brothel in an attempt to convince myself that I should know more about Maria's murder details, but in fact, I did it because of the overflowed physical pressure. It was the first time I've explored what is inside it, even though I've passed by it dozens of times.

The first time, after my conversation with some prostitutes, I forgot to ask about the incident. As soon as I was alone with one of them, she urged me to end the matter quickly. I didn't like it very much, but I found it the only way to release the frantic desires that I had from time to time. I re-convinced myself of the first argument and did it a second and a third time. When I remembered Maria, I asked one of them about her. Our bodies were just separated from each other, and when she heard Maria's name, she shivered, as if she had heard something terrifying. I tried to calm her, but she remained silent and left.

I was astonished by her reaction and the curiosity has prompted me to revisit the place and repeat the question until I found a fat girl who wasn't desired much, but she was very malicious. She didn't tell me Maria's story all at once, but in batches to force me to pay for her several times. Poor Maria, what misery you had experienced and what pain you had lived.

The expensive huge golden bracelet, which she was always wearing and cherishing because it was her only wealth, caused her to be killed by that criminal who tried to steal it after he bound and gagged her, and when he couldn't get it out of her hand he cut it and quickly fled with it. She told me that they did the impossible to save her and prayed to God to keep her alive, but she had bled a lot and died.

She sadly told me that, as if she was reminiscing about those painful moments. I don't know what this fat girl had done to become my favorite and I had often ran to her, even though she was the oldest, the least beautiful, and the fattest. She used to laugh when she saw me and lay down on the bed as if we were a married couple doing it in a usual monotony. I realized her intelligence after she told me what had happened to Maria. She had a talent for storytelling, and she used to tell me what she had known or what she had heard and had made me pay more money to extend my stay with her.

She told me about some anecdotes of what she had heard from her colleagues. I think most of them were true, and perhaps she made up the rest to draw my attention more. Her stories didn't stop and it seems that she also began to ask and collect from the others about the former prostitutes' stories secrets. I thought that sex was the direct reason for men going to the brothel, but she told me other reasons for that. Sex was indeed at the center of it, but there were also other desires that men would unload their tired bodies.

The daily work in Ezra's shop and my friend the storyteller made me forget what I had decided, so I have accepted the new situation and continued in it for several years. One day, Ezra's daughter told me of their intention to sell their house and their shop and to travel abroad. The decision wasn't surprising, as many Jews, I mean the Jews of Aleppo, had begun emigrating or thinking about it.

I went back to Damascus after a long absence. The house was needed some repairs, so I did it. It was damaged by the collapse of Sarah's house next to us, which was struck by a lightning bolt, as I was told, and burned the greater part of it. Some stones had fallen in the courtyard, and it took me several days to clean them. I yearned for the sight of plants filling the place with joy as it was in the past, so I aerated the soil before replanting it. In the meantime, I found a small pottery jar with paper inside. I know the calligraphy, it was the same I found it in the books that Sheikh Ibrahim had given to me, and they contained a few phrases that I didn't understand, it came in them:

"The safe is in Adra, and we were unable neither to bring it to Damascus nor to take it out to Beirut, so we have buried it there next to the companion's shrine."

I re-read its words, but I didn't understand anything. The letter was certainly not directed at me. He knew at that time that I couldn't leave Deir Ezzor. What did Sheikh Ibrahim mean by the safe? What is the safe? And who is it that companion's shrine? And what is he talking about? And who did he want to tell him that?

I couldn't decipher the talismans that I read. I remembered before Sheikh Ibrahim's travel, that he was busy at that time and I saw him talking with people I later knew that they were Armenians. It seemed he wrote it in a hurry. They took him to Istanbul for his cooperation with the Armenians. I remembered at the time that a rumor had circulated in Deir Ezzor that he had been executed there. Some went on about that and said that the repeated visits of these Armenians to his home weren't innocent and that something was being hatched against the Sublime State. I thanked God that I survived that, there was no doubt that if it was anything against me and would have been leaked to Yuzbashi Jamal he wouldn't have hesitated to execute me. But, who is he that companion? And what is the safe? And for whom is it?

Consequently, many questions started to come to my mind about what had happened. Oh, if the house's walls and stones would have spoken. I didn't understand anything; therefore, I folded the paper and threw it away. I didn't want to occupy myself in mazes.

While I was shopping, I noticed on the long street that there was a small closed shop. I asked about it and it was said that his heirs would like to sell it. Thus, I searched for them and spoke with their agent. I found the amount they asked for was reasonable and yet I was able to buy it for half the price that he initially offered me.

The shop was small, but it was suitable to be a barbershop. Therefore, I bought the tools that I need in my work and opened the shop. It was a nice feeling to go back to my previous work, although I paid for everything I earned in the previous years of my work, my financial situation will definitely become better.

I brought some plants and planted them in the house's garden. Then, I watered the citrus tree and pruned its dry branches, looked at it a lot, as it had used to share our morning session and breakfast with us. My father had greatly taken care of it and the small plants scattered around it. He loved mint and had planted it a lot and let it grow to emit a wonderful aroma in the house. It was as if I see him in front of me now picking its little leaves and chewing them with pleasure. I also planted jasmine and placed it on the stairs to grow and cover its edges. When my father was giving me jasmine flowers, he would say to me: You look like jasmine, pure and radiant, and your fragrance is like its scent. No, Dad, it was you who look like jasmine. You were pure and spotless, but I couldn't be, I had many mistresses and couldn't control my lusts. Yes, dad. I've done it a lot, so forgive me.

One day, I'll adjust myself and pray to the Lord and ask for his forgiveness. Then, I remembered going to the synagogue with Ezekiel. I was ashamed of myself standing in front of him. I slept with Hannah several times the previous day. I lowered my head until Ezekiel grabbed me by the hand and lead me for I was stumbling in my footsteps. I love praying in the synagogue, but I'm ashamed of the sins I had committed. Ezra used to think that I'm an atheist despite my denial of this, and this was due to the opinions I expressed in our repeated discussions.

I didn't deny that the various books that I had read have raised many questions and doubts about the entire issue of existence, but I hadn't reached the point of atheism. Yes, I used to hate the clergy, and the only exception to my dealings with a cleric was what was between me and Sheikh Ibrahim, and I think that the reason for our rapprochement was my need and addiction for culture and literature, which was what he possesses and was even unique in it until Ezekiel's appearance.

Ezekiel wasn't also a religious person, even if he pretended to be. His religion was to enjoy life until drunkenness. I didn't deny that he had an impact on me, for he was older, more knowledgeable, and had the sense of humor that I was needed in those tough days. If any problem would have emerged, Ezekiel would prepare kebab and araq; he drinks and eats greedily, without indifference to the problem facing him, and on the next day I find that the problem was completely solved; how did he do? I have no idea.

I saw with my own eyes so many results of this magic recipe and yet I didn't do it. One day, we went together to the synagogue, and, of course, that day he tried to put on the obedience's robe. However, he couldn't control himself from making some sarcastic whispers about the rabbi. We recognized that he heard it, so he hurried to show his affection and respect for the rabbi, who reluctantly accepted that.

As for Ezra, he was completely different. He was completely obedient inside and outside the synagogue, especially in the last period of his life. He wouldn't stop urging me to carry out all my religious duties, and I was then either shaking my head or finding another way to avoid completing his conversation.

Passion

Life had come to me again. An encounter I had never expected. It was she, yes, Sarah, who knocked on my door. I was surprised for my door was rarely knocked, and when I opened it, I found her in front of me in an elegant burgundy dress and a beautiful hat. Minutes have passed before I saluted her, at first I couldn't believe what I have seen. She accepted my invitation and came into the house. She had visited her family's house first and was surprised by what had happened to it. I told her that the lightning bolt had burned and destroyed the greater part of it.

We sat and talked for several hours, recalling our memories. She told me that she got married and left with her husband to Istanbul, and her mother followed her after that. She said that she didn't love him, but she also didn't hate him; she accepted him for what he was, especially after he showed interest in her mother during her severe illness. That mother who was the cause of my eternal misery. I couldn't console her for her loss. I felt that I should offer congratulations and blessings for her salvation and liberation from her, just as I had never been sad to hear the news of her husband's bankruptcy, for her mother had always dreamed to marry her like him.

She tried to control herself and keep calm while she told me the surprises that I didn't expect. She burst into tears, so I asked her permission and went shopping for her the best of what I could offer. We enjoyed the delicious food I brought. I was actually more pleased looking at her gorgeous face. She laughed and controlled me dozens of times, and I almost embrace her with my many successive looks, even though she was no longer Sarah, the teenage girl, but rather the plump and quiet lady.

We went together to her family's house. She wanted to spend the night there, but I told her it wasn't safe enough, even the room that has remained it might collapse at any moment. She intended to stay in a small motel in Damascus's city center, but I begged her to stay with me, as the house was large, and if she was embarrassed, I would leave and she would remain in the house. I was pleased she accepted to stay in the second room in my house. I understood from the small bag that she was carrying, that her visit was short and she has confirmed that later.

She intended to sell her house to pay her husband's debts in Istanbul. The reckless had risked most of his money with losing commercial speculations that led not only to his bankruptcy but also to the accumulation of debts on him, which could lead to imprisonment in the event of non-payment. She tried to hold on when she was telling the troubles that had befallen them.

I remembered Ezra's advice, so I brought some food so that we could eat together and wait for tomorrows upcoming. I admit I peeped on her while she was sleeping. Yes, I re-enjoyed the view of her body; I couldn't believe that she's actually in my home. I didn't know if she noticed and disregarded it, or if the travel harshness forced her into a deep sleep.

We had breakfast together, and she praised the beautiful plants I had planted. I should go to my work, but I didn't care. I would find an excuse for today, tomorrow, and the day after. The important thing was to stay beside her, stealing looks as much as I could from her angelic face. She urged me to find a buyer for her home as soon as possible. I went and asked many persons. The country's conditions were very difficult and the house status didn't encourage anyone to buy it. When I told her, she cried and said that she was counting on its sale amount to get out of her troubles. Her problem was confined to finding money, but my problem was my longing for her. My heart almost uttered its whim even though I know that she's a married woman and a mother and that there's a family impatiently waiting for her to come back.

I couldn't sleep that night I was looking for a solution for her, she was also worried, I realized that when I knocked on her room door to tell her that I found the solution. I told her:

- I'll mortgage my shop and give you the mortgage amount.

She was so happy when she heard my proposal, to the extent that she couldn't control herself from thanking me with successive kisses. We both wanted to find a reason to melt with a never-ending kiss, we couldn't stay away from each other, our lovely kiss forced us to stand for a long time, we mingled together; I sipped it right and I think she did the same. We exchanged kisses with wet and pliable lips, which greatly lengthened in mutual response between us. We walked to find what could comfort us until we ended up in bed, and then we sat up with the rising of our voracious kisses.

She suddenly put her hand between us after she pulled her lips from mine to pay attention to where we were. I put my head on her shoulder, despaired of distancing her hand that covered her beautiful lips. My right palm crept in and patted her left forearm, her musical tone muffled her voice from repeating the word enough, and enough is enough. I wrapped my arms around her waist, tried to stop, but I couldn't, I was drawn to her tightly and with every cell of my body from head to toe. At first, she refused to continue, so she tried to escape from me, but she couldn't. I surrounded her, pleading with everything that was between us so that we could go further.

I couldn't describe what had happened; those wonderful moments were hard to forget and words couldn't describe them. We have overlapped colors with each other to make one unique color. She was delirious and I was as well, and we let out dozens of groans as we were naked and drew very close to each other. She was concerned about the status we were in, so she tried to stop me or to stop herself. I was drunk; I admit that I was drunk with her body, which has *completely captivated me. We changed many positions, sometimes I was above her and other times she was above me, so it wasn't important; the important thing was that we were stuck to each other's bodies.*

I planted my fingers in hers, my tongue in her mouth, and I pressed my chest completely to hers until her nipples had been aroused. I tried to maintain its firmness for a few minutes as I licked as much of her upper half as I could until she opened her impenetrable walls for me. So, I penetrated her with a lust I had never known. I longed for those warm depths to complete our blending with my tongue entering her delicious mouth. My palm was roaming freely on her body, rising to her shoulders and descending to her plump buttocks when my body's lust has let out to order us to stop. We didn't care and stayed the same and continued more and more until we got tired of making love, so we stopped and separated against our will. I fell into a deep sleep, and so did she until I woke up to the screams of my body to empty the semen. When I got back from the toilet she wakes up. It seems that she was needed to empty her bodily fluids as well.

I didn't want to stop her even with a kiss my soul was eager to do. I let her go, waiting for her return impatiently, she laughed when I approached her upon her return, the laughter that my heart dances with when hearing it. I realized that abstinence no longer worked, it happened, what had happened, and we did it with all boldness and love so that she left her wonderful body for me to sip until morning.

Oh, Sarah, now I do it and I'm really pleased and satisfied. Every intercourse I did in the past was something imperfect or similar to it, and now it's actually completed. Our second intercourse had taken a long time until our bodies were revived with our lust that flowed with the accumulated love in our bodies.

It was a different morning; in fact, it was a different afternoon after we woke up to successive and wonderful kisses trying to make up for what we had missed before. I would almost publicly curse her mother, but I didn't want to spoil those wonderful moments with painful and disgusting memories. She had passed away and took with her what she had done of sins. If she wouldn't have forcibly separated us from each other, we would now be in our bed with our children next to us. I don't know why she did all this and what did she get from it? I could forgive her for keeping me away from my house, but I couldn't forgive her for keeping my love away from me. Oh, Sarah, I wished I could tell you how much I'm addicted to you. My eternal passion for you will never end.

Nonetheless, excuse me for saying: How much I hate your mother, an infinite hatred, which is the most extreme degree of hatred and disgusting, more than anyone who had hurt me in the past, even more than if they were joint all of them and dozens of times. This was how I muttered in my bed, contemplating the angelic face and remembering the reason for my misery.

I know that she would leave no matter how long she would stay, and that we might never meet again. With her wonderful touches, she took me out of the bad memories repercussions that I was in, she even excited me, and I couldn't stop myself from sticking to her and having sex with her in the house courtyard. I don't know what happened to me; it was an eroticism that I didn't witness and it was automatically renewing at every time I look at her splendor and beauty. I forced her to stick with me while I was making some food in the kitchen. We were walking together as if we were walking in endless love. Her mother had created a rift between us that can't be bridged no matter how hard we try.

Several days have passed. I only left the house to buy food for us. She reminded me again that I must hurry to mortgage my shop, as I promised her because she was late to go back to Istanbul. I was procrastinating until I had exhausted all the arguments I had invoked. Her body was so sexy, pleasurable, and a balm for all my aches, but I couldn't procrastinate anymore. I went to a usurer that one of my neighbors in the market recommended to me, and said that he was the best of them in dealing with cash. He informed me of his conditions and I accepted them, and then he gave me the money, and I took it and returned to her. She quickly put the money in her purse to the degree that I felt that she was going to leave me at once.

The next day, and upon her request, we went together to complete the procedures for selling her house to me against the mortgage money I gave to her. I didn't want what she did, but I gave in to her decision. She was in a hurry to travel, and I begged her to stay, even for a while. I proposed to her to marry, and she answered that she wanted to if it weren't for her daughter who is waiting for her return. On the night of her travel, I asked her my last request, which was a strange request for her. I wanted to tie a piece of cloth over her eyes and kiss her entire body from her head to her toe. She intended to terminate what she was in, so she agreed, and completely surrendered to me.

I started from her hair, smelling its scent, and then went down to her radiant and beautiful forehead, and then her neck and her chest. I followed this up by smelling deeply her body scent until I could feel it and it had completely entered my lungs, which had expanded a lot to contain all this fragrance. I kissed her with my lips and tasted with my tongue while my fingers press on all its body cells that I invaded with all my senses.

I went down to her waist and she let out a loud giggle and added that I tickled her in that place. I avoided it right away because there was no time to tickle, and I went on smelling and licking all her body parts. When I descended to those difficult depths, she tried to cover her with her palm, and when she realized my insistence on continuing, she let me go on with what I was in. I instructed my genitals to give her unforgettable memories; so it eagerly responded to me. Thus, I repeated it more and more; I hoped the time would stop for a little to taste everything I wanted from her body.

The Bitter Departure

The departure hour is ticking; I hated it a lot, but she had to leave, and my body cells were almost rebelling against me and following her against my will. Several days had passed and I was reliving those wonderful moments. In fact, it is the only happiest event that I had ever known in my entire life, but as for the rest of them, I think they were misery and sadness. Her body is beautiful, very sexy, despite her marriage and pregnancy; even her breasts are beautiful with their pink nipples. Sarah, is a legend of beauty, with all that she's, and no woman in the universe could be compared to her and her beauty. I searched for her all over Aleppo. I hoped to meet whatever woman might look like her, but I didn't find her. Even Maria, who I thought might look like her, wasn't more than a mirage, and then a prostitute and later a killed.

I have had to work day and night to pay off the mortgage, thus I tried to decrease my monthly expenses to the minimum. I was hungry only for reading, I used to buy some old books and resell them after finishing them. I reduced my going to the coffee shop to hear the storyteller and enjoy a cup of tea accompanying his endless stories despite my love for hearing those historical stories. The storyteller would sit at the front of the coffee shop and we would gather to interact with the story events, which he impersonates by changing the tone of his voice and amplifying it and some interactive movements of his hands.

He was mastering the storytelling to the degree that some would refuse to return to his home before he knows the story's end. I witnessed some quarrels where the audience was divided between supporters and opponents of a character in it, and sometimes, to avoid the recurrence of such problems, the storyteller was inventing other endings for his story.

I used to spend most of my time in my small shop, which dispensed me about false and useless relationships, so I stayed in it to do my work, and I often use to have my breakfast there. It wasn't a full breakfast, but rather a loaf of tandoori bread with a glass of milk, and sometimes I use to replace the milk with a piece of local cheese or soft cottage cheese with which I start my day before the customers come in. My lunch was also simple, with no timing for it according to my free time from the last customer who came to me.

Sometimes I use to take a simple outing in the old streets, and then to Al-Nawfara Coffee shop to sit in it, enjoying the water descending like the cascade. It was a breathtaking and fresh sight. I used to restrain myself from going to the coffee shop next to it so that I wouldn't have to go every day to hear the rest of the storyteller's story.

I used to decrease more on my expenses, as the usurer, from whom I got the mortgage money, has warned me of the necessity of periodically paying off. Sarah's body was still stuck in my mind with all its details. Why didn't she accept my proposal to marry her? As long as she couldn't bear her husband, as she said, he is a drunkard, a gambler, and perhaps impotent, and perhaps she was ashamed to declare that. What would she benefit from him? I was dazed, so I returned home after I wandered on many basalt stones roads. I dream of her coming back to me. I did everything in my power to make her happy, and I wouldn't have intended to buy her home for what I gave her if it didn't for her insistence on it.

She was as I had known her, respectful and classy, and what happened between us was nothing more than eternal love. We didn't cheat on her husband. He was the one who invaded our world with his arrogance and recklessness. She's mine and I'm hers. As for that crazy husband, he's an annoyance we are used to from her mother. I'm sure that she would return so that we could go on with our love and on the same bed. Oh, Sarah, how much I would be happy if you would come back to me so that we could spend the rest of our life sipping our joys. Poor Sarah, what hell are you living in now? You live with a sick daughter, a gambler's husband, and extreme poverty. I wished you would come back to me. I paid off the third due payment. I was happy that I did it on time and without delay, thanks to the cupping that I had performed a lot and the medicinal herbs that I had sold to my customers. I went home, tired, and lay down on the bed that was once the stage for a pleasure that has lasted until morning.

My mother-in-law's sudden illness stopped me from completing the scrolls reading. She had a slight cold at first, but it increased until it forced her to stay in her bed. My father-in-law asked her to rest, but she didn't take care of herself and proceeded to wash the wool quilts that we use for sleeping; she spread them in the open air, and then put them back after upholstering them again. She considered that some works are accurate and important, so she was insisting that she performs them herself due to her expertise, which she often brags about. My youngest son was suffering from nocturnal urination and although I used to put an extra piece of cloth under him and wash it in the morning, my mother-in-law has insisted to wash the entire mattress with its wool filling. We showed him to a doctor who had given him the right medicine, but sometimes he urinates at night.

Influenza has afflicted my mother-in-law so hard to the degree that she found it difficult to go to the toilet on her own. She was leaning on me until the door, but she was insisting on entering it alone. She's shy by nature. I told her: There is nothing wrong with the patient, for you're my mother. Nonetheless, she thanked me and prayed for me, and insisted on entering it alone. I know that she was longing for her home and her friends and that she was living in depression as our current situation is depressing and critical; but we were all suffering too, as we were forcibly displaced and left behind all the beautiful memories.

I covered her with a thick blanket after she lay down in her bed, for she was feeling cold, and let out some groans that she wasn't used to except when she was very sick.

I wished her fast recovery, out loud, and she looked at me deeply, and then embraced me with clear motherly affection. I brought her a diet dish of boiled potatoes with a little of olive oil; my father-in-law soon shared it with her so that I had to peel the second batch of it and put it in the plate that my father-in-law had emptied.

I took advantage of their side conversations to go back to reading the scrolls, but I quickly stopped as the children were back from school and I had to serve the food I had prepared for them. Therefore, I postponed the reading until the next day and have preoccupied with their playing and their endless requests.

I don't know what prompted me to do that. I was on my house rooftop inspecting it, and I went down from it to Sarah's house, or rather, which was Sarah's house. I went down slowly, because its condition had become frightening and dilapidated, and was about to fall at any moment. I stood in its courtyard, which was once her mother's favorite place to receive her guests. I came into it through the small door and tried to check it. The stones had smashed most of its wooden furniture. It was difficult to repair; it should be demolished and rebuilt again. No one might want it in its present condition, I might do it one day when I would have the money for it, but I won't sell it. I'll rebuild it again as it was before and sit on the rooftop and look at it to relive those old days.

I noticed that there was a small notebook, so I took it with me. I liked the plants that I had planted, as the view was wonderful from the rooftop. I'll bring more plants and put them in every corner of it, and I'll bring some animals with me to comfort me and dispel my loneliness. But what kind of animals should I bring? Maybe a monkey! No, no, it's impossible.

I laughed as I had remembered the monkey I had seen earlier in Aleppo. He made everyone laugh. The monkey is distinguished from other animals in that he always has new actions. But what animal, can I bring that doesn't need special care? I just want to be entertained by such plants as I see them and admire their appearance and their silence. No animal is silent. The lamb needs daily food and cleaning, as well as chicken. I'll indeed benefit from them, but I can't take care of them. I reviewed all the pets; they all need attention and care. I think only the turtle is like the plant, silent and isolated. It will eat the leaves and plants that I had overgrown in the indoor pots and their residues had become fertilizer for the soil. Yes, I'll bring it soon, and I also need a lot of books, as I'm tired of re-reading the same books. I had memorized them all, and there is no book that I hadn't read more than its author himself. I think I can write. Yes, I must try. But about what should I write? I don't know, I'll think deeply about it, and for a long time.

It was a normal day I spent in my shop, rather it was a normal week, a normal month and a normal year, this is how life goes on and we repeat our actions. But the important thing is that on this day I paid off the full mortgage amount. Now, no more debts would bother me. And I'll never do it again.

Sarah was worth it. I indeed worked for a long time and my obsession was to pay off what was due, but I think that what I had paid was an understatement for what I had got. I'll never be able to forget those wonderful moments that had extended until the morning. If we would have gotten married after that, it would have been the honeymoon that precedes the marriage, and we might have followed it with other honeymoon months if she had accepted! I wasn't bothered by her justification, as I know that some things are difficult to be attained.

She was different from any woman I had known. They were indeed like her in some matters; they knew men before, and I wasn't the first man in their lives who made them lose their virginity; however, she remains a different woman from them, who didn't do it with vulgarity and immorality. We were like a married couple spending cordially and with love an intimate night on their bed. Delicious were those minutes and had an eternal meaning as all my *body cells were saturated with her wonderful body flavor. I let my eyes free to peep on her seductive body and let my tongue taste it. My five senses had sipped and merged with her senses.*

If the mortgage amount would have required me to work my whole life, I would do without hesitation, for she really deserves it. If Sarah would come back, I would give her everything, just to be together. Sarah was my first and only love. I tried to find an alternative similar to her so that I used to go to those places where women's bodies were offered at different prices according to specific criteria. I didn't deny that they were different among themselves, but Sarah's the whole difference. She has boobs and buttocks similar to theirs, except that she's different. I don't know in what? But she's different.

When she would speak, a distinguished rhythm was flowing from her lips, forcing me to listen to her, and when she offered me her body to be touched with my fingertips, she offered me a rare painting that I have to look at for a long time and touch it very carefully. She's a crystal master unique piece. Oh, Sarah, if you're with me now to let's sip each other in a renewed eroticism moment. My curses will continue to haunt your mother in her grave. If she would have known what she did to us and what she sinned against us. I would still forever launching many curses as I could, hoping that one day they would reach and stone her with all hatred and bitterness. I bought the needed papers, and I'll start writing my pains and the events that I had gone through, to the degree that some might not believe, as they are like the tales of Sinbad.

I put the turtle I found by the river under the citrus tree. She hid at first in her shell, and then soon began to wander around the plants' pot, exploring it. I was pleased with her slow steps and hiding in the grass. Then I felt the presence of a new very kind and witty guest. My happiness was to stay at home, and I could no longer afford to leave it except for rare occasions or to purchase the necessities. I was pleased with an offer from someone I had never known before. The offer was attractive and I couldn't refuse it. Why do I need a shop and work? And what he paid may guarantee me a good living for the rest of my life. I'll read and read exactly as Ezekiel had advised me and also write what I had drawn from my experiences in this life. I hid the money that I had got as the price of selling the shop. It's my wealth that will preserve my dignity. I wished Sarah would come back and we live together in my house, and read her the most beautiful stories and spend the night practicing our eternal love.

How much I miss you and I love your eyes with their different and lovely looks. Come, my love, I have enough for us and we won't need anything else. You're everything to me. You're Damascus with its lanes, with its beautiful river, and its adjacent houses. You're the earth with its fragrance and the sky with its purity. You're everything. I'm still waiting for you. When does your heart yearn for me? Quit him, he's a drunken man and heavily indebted. What's your need for semi-man? Come to me, I'm your first boyfriend, lover, and eternal husband. I wish if you would have agreed to that.

I was so tired I didn't respond to the noise that he tried to wake me up with. I knew that he would be late to come back home, as he informed me that he might go with his friends to see a movie in the cinema. He lay down next to me, I felt him, but I disregarded him. He kissed me, but I didn't move; he whispered in my ear that he brought me something delicious to eat together, I also didn't care. I was completely drowsy, and usually, when I get to this moment the happiest thing for me is to sleep. I realized that he was aroused when he got close to me. Then, he got closer to me until I could feel him completely. I wished if he had postponed this until the next morning or evening.

He came in so late, and he had got enough pleasure of watching a movie with his friends. As for me, I spent most of my time in tiring work until the children had gone to bed. I felt his hands trying to bare my buttocks. I turned my back to him, but I didn't prevent him; I didn't want to spoil his desire. He also bared his lower part and approached me more. He tried for the last time to arouse me with his fingertips, but I didn't respond to him. I felt him approaching me, but my sleeping position hindered him, so I bent my left knee more to allow him to move on. He realized what I did, so he kissed me again, hoping that we could do it together. After despairing to attract me to have sex, he penetrated me with a swift and violent movement. Then I gave him more relief so that he could complete what he was in, but with some calm and away from the repulsive sounds of his body colliding with mine.

Perhaps he realized that and tried to fix it well, I don't know whether he deliberately disregarded it or was he busy cleaning his body after his lust was extinguished, so he left my buttocks bared for a while until he realized that and he fixed it. I didn't reproach him in the morning, and I didn't even show my astonishment at what I found on my body from his body traces, but rather I expressed to him my regret that I was tired.

He was unusually silent, and there was no reaction from him. Silence and apathy have fallen upon us for several days, during which I didn't want to disturb him with anything, until one day he came in with the papers I had requested and some books that he had borrowed from his friends.

His nights with his friends would bother me and I was never used to him staying out of the house for a long time. I preferred and even wanted we stay close to each other and talk before we went to sleep, but he's no longer the same, he has changed a little; they were urgent changes that caught my attention recently.

Finally, we went to the Rabwa region, as Fahd had promised us. It was a wonderful outing on the Barada riversides. My father-in-law was very happy and so was my mother-in-law, who showed finally her satisfaction. She started telling us about her childhood and youth, so my father-in-law would interfere when she starts to list some of their privacy, as she's eager to reveal everything in her heart. I laughed encouragingly while my husband was very reserved. With her usual intelligence, she moved on to other topics so that our happiness wouldn't be spoiled.

We went back home very tired. The children quickly fell asleep after their long-playing, and it seems that my father-in-law also sent his encrypted messages to my mother-in-law, and they went together to their little nest. We, too, were desiring to complete our happiness with an intimate encounter, so we did it with great passion. He assured me that what he went through was nothing more than a passing summer cloud. He eagerly hugged me naked until I felt his body infiltrating inside me.

It was a wonderful dream that brought me together with Sarah, and I wished it was true, it made me happy all day to the point that I imagined more than once hearing knocks on the door, to find out later that it wasn't true. Sarah had come with her beauty to me, we had slept together in one bed and made love more than once. I didn't feel sorry for her like before because I was sure that she would be back very soon and very soon. It's only a matter of time and I have to prepare for this encounter. Only political matters were bothering me. I started feeling changes in the faces. I have heard many warnings from my Jews' neighbors and friends not to leave the neighborhood because some were inflaming the feelings against the Jews, and there may be angry reactions from others against us.

I didn't show much interest in what was said at the beginning. I focused on completing the writing on my scrolls and waiting for the return of my beloved Sarah. Otherwise, I didn't care too much. Other people's reactions and looks confirmed to me the warnings' credibility I had heard. Therefore, I responded against my will to those fears and postponed the idea of rebuilding Sarah's house until her return, and I didn't leave my house unless necessary. I wished if Sarah was beside me, how much I need her now!!!

I spent a whole day very sick in my bed, something like numbness was creeping into my whole body little by little, and I couldn't move after that. I was in the basement at the time when I heard screaming from outside and murmurs, followed by violent knocks at the house door. I couldn't know the source because of my severe illness.

The next morning I went to the doctor, who had advised me to get a complete rest, and I did. The lemonade has refreshed my tired body. I have to get married, I can't spend the rest of my life like this waiting for Sarah; it seems like she won't come back, but what if she did? Yes, it may come back. She was tired like me. She may surprise me with her visit, and she may even ask me about my wife. She wouldn't believe that I got married. No, no, I won't do it. I'll be patient. I'll wait for her to come back. She'll definitely come back. Yes, she'll definitely come back. This is what my heart always tells me, and even all my body cells.

I had tougher days more than these before, but they had passed. This is how the days will pass with their sweetness and their bitterness, and only patience will make the results differ. More than a week passed and I had run out of everything, so I went out to buy my spiritual and physical needs. I rewarded my patience with a large piece of kunafa that I had devoured to the last. I brought with me a large box of sweets and a lot of dates as well as nuts and dried fruits; I adore them for their intense taste, so I used to buy large quantities to keep for a long time. Vague murmurs were revolving around me. I heard them getting closer and closer and then moving away. Some of them came from the house that I had bought from Sarah, and some of them had come from the house courtyard. I went up to the rooftop but didn't see anything that caught my attention. I checked all the house rooms, even the smaller kitchen, only there was complete silence in the basement. I slept a quiet night and was able to re-read the book "The Animal", a book that I'll never get bored of.

I went out again to get what I was needed. I don't know what was going on? Weird faces I had never seen before. I passed on my way to my previous shop. The new owner was completely occupied with his work, and I didn't want to interrupt him. I wished I hadn't sold it. Damn greed, it tempted me with what he paid me. It was indeed said: "The seller is the loser." But I didn't lose much, I bought a house for a quarter of its price, I'll fix it and sell it. It indeed needs a lot, so what happened to it made it unfit except for demolition and rebuilding.

When Sarah had visited me, I hesitated to discuss with her the subject of my forced expulsion from Damascus. Therefore, I hinted to her, but I found that she didn't know anything about the subject except that it was an order that had to be carried out, and she disproved the rumors I had told her. She said that her mother didn't tell her anything, and if she was the reason, she would have known for her. She was completely convinced of her mother's innocence; I wished I had the same conviction that she had.

The strange murmurs have returned to the house, so I went down to the basement and slept a calm night away of fear. In the morning, I went up to the rooftop; I saw a strange movement, but it was far away, so I hastily got down for fear of it. Only the citrus tree heard my whispers, and the turtle joined us with her strange facial features as if she wanted to listen to my words, so I gave her the remained food to eat. I didn't know what these sounds were that interfere in my ears from time to time. I was sure someone wanted to hurt us.

There was a lot of gossip about it until it became the most important talk. Last week, I listened to a conversation among a group of elderly people, who were the neighborhood's residents. One of them, who was the oldest, spoke of Jews' massacres that took place during the Shavuot feast celebrations in Iraq, and that there were thousands of wounded and dead and nearly a thousand houses were completely destroyed. I saw anxiety and fear in their eyes that I had never seen before, so I felt a shiver in my body similar to the one I had in the past. That day, I hurried back to my house and lockdown on myself.

My father told me about the persecution that our ancestors were subjected to in Spain, which had forced them to leave it. I remembered most of those stories that my father had told me, so I feared more. If my father had been present, he would have relieved my mounting fear, and if Sarah had been present, we would certainly have forgotten our fear by making love repeatedly.

I think she's on her way to me; she had been gone for a long time. I wish I know her conditions now, as well as Ezekiel and Hannah's conditions, how much I wish they would be fine, and that the news coming from Iraq would be false rumors. The good days will soon pass. I wish we had stayed in Aleppo, that city that includes all *kinds of pleasures. I'll never forget those years I had spent there. Ezekiel had bestowed me a friendship that I longed for, despite the big difference in age between us. Likewise, Hannah is, although our character was very different.*

Ezekiel told me stories about some of our clergymen's hypocrisy and of all sects as well. Thus, I had hated them all. He had many real stories about what he had heard about them, and he was happy to expose their other side with their desires and instincts. At first, I didn't believe everything he had told until I found out that he was the secret box in which the prostitutes have deposited their sexual relations secrets. It's the body itself with all its organs and cells either it was for the normal man, or the master, or the clergyman who fills our ears with empty preaching. The hidden world is our inferior natures' mirror, which we are always keen to hide.

I went out to wander the streets of Damascus looking for something that would make me forget my loneliness, but I came back empty-handed, even my home became scary at times, except for the basement, which I had arranged to be a comfortable refuge when needed. I slept deeply after reading an old manuscript I have recently purchased.

In the morning, I watered all the plants, as well as the citrus tree, which stands tall and whose leaves provide food for the turtle. I looked at her; she hid shyly at first, and then reappeared as if she remembered me, so she felt secure. I went up to the rooftop to relax in the sun and noticed that there were other stones in the courtyard and that seem to have collapsed recently. I was terrified by their large number as if the wall would collapse, but it seems that the house would be begun to collapse. I'll try to get someone to demolish it so that its old stones don't fall next to my basement hole.

It seems that f Sarah's mother's spirit appeared in the house after learning that I had bought it. Of course, she wouldn't have accepted, and would never have sold it to me. There is no doubt that her bones are now grinding and fighting because of hearing that news. I wish she would come after I would reconstruct it and she would see me sitting in her favorite place where she used to sit. I wish I could see her eyes. Oh, what joy! It's equivalent to all the sadness and misery I have been through because of her, yes. I wish she would see me smiling and victorious in her house, or rather the house that I bought from my beloved, her daughter Sarah.

I brought more papers; I want to write everything down. My father said it to me before when we were in the synagogue, and I asked him about the scrolls that day, and he replied, "The Holy Books." I liked them very much, as it was a different way of writing and reading from the book, so I chose it to write down everything that had happened with me on that journey that I took in life. When I re-read what I wrote, I stopped at the difficult moments I went through, and I felt that words have failed to describe the whole truth. Perhaps I forgot some of them... What I could remember I'll re-write to complete my story with all its sorrows chapters. I moved some of the needed books to the basement to enjoy reading them while I would be lying down on the bed that I had arranged there. I used to feel safer here, in this wonderful space that gives me more serenity feeling and belonging to the place.

I disagreed with my father only on this point. I didn't know why he hated it. I rarely ever saw him enter it or inspect it. I was the only one who was putting some things and food supplies in it. Sometimes, I considered it the safer place to encounter Sarah away from all gazes. I would prefer the far inner corner in which we used to rediscover our bodies' secrets. We used to spend pleasant moments, and when we would hear my father's voice calling me, I would go out and would invoke all the arguments to him.

I think he had known what was going on and perhaps he considered it a childish pastime and nothing more, although it was bigger and deeper. When Sarah visited me after we had made love for the third time, she asked me to go down to the basement and check it out. She, too, yearned for those innocent, childish moments between us. She reminded me of what I used to do with her and I reminded her of what she was doing to me. It was one of the most pleasant times we have had sex together, and perhaps it was the same as the second time, *in the same place and the same way. We felt that we had completed our love, so there was no fear of hearing her mother screaming while she was looking for her around their house, nor for my father's voice that could come searching for me. I kept the bed that we carried together there, so there was no doubt that she will return after she would complete the divorce proceedings from that thing called her husband.*

I no longer heard much of those murmurs that I used to hear, and the days had accelerated while I was immersing in writing and reading. I didn't know that writing is so amazing until I practiced it. It became an indispensable daily ritual; the reading preceded and was the pleasure that relieved me of what I was in. Of course, my pleasure would have been complete if I had read a little and made love with Sarah a lot, and then re-read wonderful books while I could be in the arms of the most wonderful body.

The days have quickly passed. I had to check the other house after I had heard the sound of some stones falling. The house was in scary condition so I thought of selling it. I showed it to one of my acquaintances, who surprised me with his response. He told me: Many Jews had secretly begun to leave the country, and that no one would want to buy a new house, but on the contrary, everyone wishes to sell. The mystery was surrounding what was happening here, and he added that he had also planned to travel soon, and he asked me not to reveal the secret so that he wouldn't be exposed to any unnecessary problem; I promised him to keep the secret, and he advised me to leave the country as soon as possible, so I didn't say a word. I repeated my offer to another person, and his answer was similar to what I had heard before. After repeatedly hearing the same answer, I realized that the conditions weren't any more appropriate for selling. Therefore, I expelled the idea from my head and replaced it with another solution. I decided to demolish the house because its situation was getting worse day by day and hoping to build a new house in the future.

I tried to take a break from the thinking that has troubled me, for I had blamed myself a lot for buying a house in such a miserable condition and might fall at any moment. I got back to writing. There was still a lot that I went through that I need to write down. While I was engrossing in my writing, I heard a strong and disturbing sound that frightened me, coinciding with the fall of stones. I checked what happened. I don't know what was going on? I no longer saw the staircase entrance. I cried out loud. I don't know what to do, I sat thinking, and then I continued writing. But, I have to go out first.

I'm going to sleep a little so I can find a solution to my problem tomorrow, I can't breathe, I screamed, what should I do? What do I do? No, I won't die here I screamed again Sarah save me, Sarah save me, please, please save me I'm here down in the same place you know, save me, save me, Sarah, please, Sarah…..

He was surprised by my question and he didn't answer. I answered on his behalf. I told him: There was a corpse in the basement. He looked at me with shock on his face. He didn't answer but remained silent that provocative silence. Only his looks were distracting the answer. I would have screamed at him but I wasn't used to it. With tears in my eyes, I said: Tell me please, was there a corpse in the basement? He asked me to lower my voice first, then said in a voice closer to a whisper: I'll tell you everything, calm down, calm down, but first I want you to promise me not to say what I'll say. I replied: I do. He looked into my eyes when I answered, and then added, after bringing the Book of God: Put your hand on the Qur'an and swear. I told him: Didn't you believe me; I told you I'll keep your secret. He said: Yes, but to calm my heart. I put my hand on the Qur'an and swore as he wanted. He returned in his low voice: Yes, there was a corpse, and my father asked me to take it out and bury it away and to conceal the matter. You know my mother's sensitivity to the subject. She wouldn't accept staying here if she knew about it and the house, as you know, was hard-earned. He had passed away and nothing is frightening. I was aware that he had enough arguments for what he did, so I didn't want to go further. I only blamed him for keeping such an important secret from me.

I couldn't understand many of the words in the last pages that he had written and they were rather vague. Just some words and letters and scribbles following Sarah's name, which he repeated over and over again. It seems that he wrote it after he had despaired of someone coming to save him. I tried to decipher those talismans, but I couldn't, it was clear that they were just a person's emotional lines taking his last breath.

I asked my husband to let me visit the basement. He hesitated at first and then agreed. We went down together after he removed the stones that closed its iron gate. He entered before me because he was afraid of some reptiles. It was like a stone cave, another world different from the rest of the house. I examined its corners, especially the one in which he has isolated himself to write down his secrets life, and at the same time witnessed his pleasure and his end.

I noticed my husband's astonishing looks. I told him in the past some of what I had read, but he asked me to stop until it was finished, so he knows little about the subject. My fingers touched its stones and came close to the wall to the point of sticking. I hoped that these huge and compact stones would complete the details of his ending so that I could finally understand what he had written, but the place was able to swallow all the secrets it had witnessed. I agreed with my husband after his insistence and we went out together. He let out a loud sigh after leaving. I don't know if it was spontaneous or intentional to draw my attention to what he had felt below.

I went back to the scrolls, read what they said hoping to found the missing episodes that would complete the rest of the events for me. My husband listened to me and I read to him what came in it.

He was urging me to narrate it orally until it ends quickly, while I hoped that he would share with me a reading of what was stated in it, hoping that he would find out through that what I couldn't understand. We found a middle ground between us, a quick read, and a brief comment. He was in a hurry to complete it as quickly as possible, and I asked more of my questions to win from him a correct analysis of what he understood of the story. Kislev had suffered persecution and oppression to the point of suffocation. He lost his mother and his only childhood friend, and then his father, and then his only love. They forcibly took him into the unknown, without he could realize what he had committed. He only had to obey and implement without objection or even without thinking. I wished he had written and explained more about what he was going through in his last days. His sentences were crude and vague and at times only revealed a specific angle of what he had been through. He mastered writing down his pain and his sorrows, and he didn't disregard to describe the happy and hopeful moments that were scarce, and which were a drop in his miserable sea.

The children came back from school and I had to hurry to serve them food. I won't be able to tell them the story of Kislev, and the mystery of his corpse existence will remain a secret between us, as I promised my husband, so that my children's smiles won't disappear and they would be overwhelmed by fear and panic over what happened earlier in the house.

My father-in-law's decision was right to close the basement permanently. We will never use it. It was one day a grave for a man who started his life as an orphan who his mother died before she could breastfed him her milk. He died alone in grief and lamentation over memories that had never left him. One day we'll leave this house, and then I'll tell my children and perhaps my grandchildren the Scrolls of Kislev story.